Changing Gears

Shifting into Love: Book One

Roseanne Beck

COPYRIGHT

CHANGING GEARS
Copyright © 2019 Roseanne Beck

Cover by Fresh Design

DEDICATION

For Karla

Thank you for keeping me grounded while encouraging me to stretch my wings.

ACKNOWLEDGEMENTS

Thank you to everyone who has helped me in this most exciting journey.

I have an amazing group of critiquers and beta readers. Although there are too many of you to name, I couldn't have done this without you. A special shout out to the Marbles, who not only helped me find the plot but also provided endless encouragement and cheerleading.

And of course, I thank *you*, the reader. Thank you for taking a chance on a new author. I truly appreciate your time and energy.

Changing Gears

CHAPTER ONE

Lauren

As I scan the karaoke bar, I'm certain of several things.

One—Mullet Mike should absolutely be banned from wearing Elvis jumpsuits.

Two—the older women who always commandeer the front-center table have the bluest hair I've ever seen.

And three—the couple onstage performing *I Got You Babe* make a very convincing Sonny and Cher. Even though they're both men.

What I'm not certain of is the location of my sister. Or her boyfriend, AJ. They were supposed to meet us here half an hour ago.

As if reading my mind, my friend Megan asks, "Where's Kylie?"

I shrug. "Who knows? Maybe she and AJ are stuck at work."

Megan swivels toward me and raises an eyebrow. "Yeah. Stuck licking each other's faces off."

"Ew. Thanks for that mental picture." Although she's right. That probably *is* what they're doing. And I have actually caught them doing worse. Much, much worse. On the counters of our shop, no less.

I'm totally scarred for life.

Not that I'm a prude or anything. But you're not supposed to see your sister *in flagrante*. Ever. Definitely not at your place of business. And definitely not with an employee. Although, of the two of us, she would be the one to push the boundaries.

"Oh! There she is. Hey, Kylie! Over here!" Megan waves toward the front door, then drops her voice. "Uh-oh. She looks pissed."

Crap. She does look pissed. My sister's movements are clipped and rigid, she's got that steely look in her eye, and I can practically see the steam coming out of her ears.

"Everything okay?" I ask as she plunks her butt on the barstool next to me.

"No, Lauren," Kylie spits out. "Everything is *not* okay. Where's Andrew?" She cranes her neck, trying to locate the bartender.

Oookay. Megan and I share a glance, and I slide my glass of Shiraz in front of Kylie.

My sister pulls a face and pushes the glass back toward me. "No thanks. I need the hard stuff tonight." She catches Andrew's eye. "I need a Three Wise Men!"

Megan lets out a low whistle, and my eyes widen. Kylie hasn't done shots of Johnnie Walker,

Jim Beam, and Jack Daniels for a long time. I don't even think Dad's death rated that particular trifecta.

Kylie slides a credit card across the counter, slams back the drink Andrew places in front of her, and then motions for another. "Just start a tab."

Megan and I exchange another glance before I turn my attention back to my sister. "So, uh, what brings your three favorite guys back to town?"

Kylie presses her lips into a thin line, and her nostrils flare. Sure signs that she's trying hard not to explode. She knocks back her second shot and winces. "Damn. That's good." She blows out a long breath, either trying to calm herself down or negate the alcohol sting, and her knuckles whiten around her shot glass. "AJ and I are done."

"Oh, Ky." I throw my arm around her shoulders and pull her in for a quick hug. "I'm so sorry." I know it's the right thing to say, but a tiny piece of me breathes a sigh of relief. I never thought he was good enough for her. There was just something about him that rubbed me the wrong way. But now is definitely not the time to tell her that.

Again.

Of course, the fact that they're no longer together also means the atmosphere at the shop will be *super* uncomfortable. After all, he is our chief bicycle mechanic.

Great.

"What happened?" I ask.

"He started acting weird yesterday. Found him freaking out this afternoon."

Megan and I share a glance. AJ has the emotional range of a teaspoon. I wouldn't have

thought freaking out was in his wheelhouse. Unless…
"He wasn't on drugs, was he?" God. That would
explain so much.

"What? No." Kylie shakes her head. "Turns out,
he got a call from his ex." Her jaw clenches. "His
pregnant ex."

"Oh. Wow." At least it's not Kylie who's
pregnant. That's a whole other level of complication
we just can't handle right now.

"Wait," Megan says. "Is he—"

"—the father? Yep." Kylie cracks her knuckles.

"Huh. Guess he's not such a bad guy after all," I
muse.

Kylie's nostrils flare, and she's gripping her
glass so tightly I wouldn't be surprised to see it
shatter. "She wasn't pregnant when AJ and I started
dating."

Megan cringes. "Oh, shit."

"Yeah. He was cheating on me with his ex."
Kylie takes several deep breaths and straightens her
shoulders. "Anyway. I've decided."

"That you're not gonna date any more losers?"
Crap. Didn't mean to say that out loud. Must've been
a combination of the wine and stress.

She shoots me with her laser beam eyes. "No.
Well, yes. But no. No more dating for me, period.
And definitely no dating employees. For either of us.
Too messy."

I bite back a snort. I could've told her that. Hell,
I *did* tell her that. On several occasions. But
mentioning that fact now isn't gonna do either of us
any good.

And while part of me resents her feeling the need to include me in her decree, the majority of my brain shrugs in resignation. Not like it's gonna be a hardship on my end. I don't recall the last time I went out on a date. Even before our dad's death six months ago, dating and I never really got along. Partially because I'm naturally introverted, and partially because I'm socially awkward around hot guys. Add in the fact that I'm still trying to sort through the shop's finances while working part-time at the college, and I've got my hands full.

Plus, our only other employee is our uncle. "Crap! Uncle Pete!"

Kylie waves her hand. "Eh, I don't think Uncle Pete's gonna miss AJ. He never did like him very much."

"No. I mean, isn't Uncle Pete's shoulder surgery tomorrow?"

"Yeah." Her eyes widen. "Shit. I totally forgot about that."

"Please tell me AJ's ex lives locally."

Kylie shakes her head. "He quit. He's probably at the airport now."

"What?" I squeak. "He didn't even give us notice? Can you call him and beg him to stay?" Not that I really want AJ hanging around, but with him gone and Uncle Pete out of commission for several weeks, we'll have zero bicycle mechanics. Which isn't really a good business model for a bicycle shop. Especially one that's already struggling.

While Kylie has the skills to do repairs, her days are usually jam-packed with the front-end aspects of the job—customer service, ordering supplies and equipment, trying to get a handle on the overall business. And I'm just the numbers girl—finances, accounts payable, and accounts receivable. Totally hopeless when it comes to the hands-on stuff.

Kylie huffs. "Hell, no, I am not begging him to stay. We'll figure something out. We always do."

I swallow the rest of my drink in one long gulp.

We'd better figure it out. And quick. I've run the numbers. Things don't look pretty.

There's a $10,000 estate tax due in a couple of months and a $30,000 balloon payment due several months after that. Which we might be able to cover with some hard work and a little luck.

Timing-wise, the beginning of spring always brings an increase in bike sales and repairs. Plus, the upcoming Pedals & Medals event usually results in a bump in the income column. Add in the new City Bike Program we've been hearing whispers about and Dad's life insurance policy, and we might just be able to squeak by.

Assuming, of course, we have a mechanic.

Geez. I didn't think I could dislike my sister's latest boyfriend any more.

I guess I was wrong.

After another glass of wine, however, things don't seem quite so bad.

Except my sister's singing. That's still as horrible as ever. Some people get better as their blood alcohol level rises. Not Kylie. It starts at "tone deaf" and goes downhill from there. She's currently in her "dying cat" range.

What she lacks in the ability to hit any kind of recognizable pitch, she more than makes up for with enthusiasm, however. That's part of what makes her so good at her job. I would much rather be behind the scenes. She, on the other hand, doesn't mind making them.

Karaoke's probably one of the few places I'm okay being in the spotlight, especially after a couple of drinks, and especially when Kylie's onstage with me. Because one—as opposed to my sister, I actually have a decent voice. And two—with her up there, it's a safe bet no one will be paying much attention to me.

Which is why I don't protest when she waves me up.

"You two have fun!" Megan chuckles as she shoos me away.

A grin stretches across my face when I see the song Kylie has queued up. Taking the extra mic from her outstretched hand, I mentally prepare myself for the performance of one of our old standbys. I manage to maintain my focus until Kylie starts gyrating to the disco beat of Gloria Gaynor's *I Will Survive*.

Damn. Every time. My sister always manages to do something to throw me off. It's like her superpower. This time, she's doing a weird combination of the disco finger point and the wax on/wax off maneuver from *The Karate Kid*, all while swiveling her hips as if she's trying to win a hula-hoop contest.

After the third time she bumps her hip against mine, I give in. It's either join her or sustain massive bruising.

So I join her with the disco pointy finger and rock my hips side to side.

If disco wasn't dead before, we sure are killing it now.

And not in a good way.

But the crowd seems to be enjoying it. The Blue Hair Ladies even shout with us as we butcher the chorus and disco-point toward the door.

And despite the fact that I'm actually a pretty good singer, my voice slides right off the note. Because there, right inside the door, is one of the most gorgeous guys I've ever seen. Dark hair that's a little too long to be considered respectable, tattoos snaking up muscular forearms. The only imperfection is the fact that he's on crutches, a huge green cast extending from under his shorts down to his toes.

Well, that, and the scowl on his face.

But even the scowl looks sexy.

Just adds to the bad boy appearance.

The scowl deepens as Kylie hits a note that makes even me cringe. And I've had a lifetime of building up my immunity.

His eyes flick to mine, and electricity races down my spine.

Of course, that could be my nervous system trying to reboot itself after Kylie's misfire.

Okay, Lauren. Focus. You're here to support your sister. Not pick up men.

Ha! As if.

Picking up men is Megan's thing. Just like being the tomboy extrovert is Kylie's thing and being the introverted good girl is mine.

Plus, he's here with a woman. And even if he wasn't, he looks like he'd be right up Megan's alley. And definitely out of my league.

So, I refocus on my sister, catching her eye in time to belt out the final line. While I'm still holding the note, she shouts, "Suck it, AJ!"

"That's right!" one of the Blue Hair Ladies yells back. "You tell him!"

Fearing that Kylie might, in fact, continue to tell AJ just what he can do, I wrestle the mic out of her hand and sling an arm around her shoulder, forcibly leading her off the stage.

"I *will* survive," she slurs as I steer her back toward our seats. "Without AJ. Without men! Men!" She throws back her head and barks out a laugh. "We don't need no stinking men!"

My heart stutters as we pass by Mr. Hottie's table.

Need? No.

But it sure would be nice to have the option once in a while.

CHAPTER TWO

Jake

"Seriously? I make one innocent comment about getting bed sores from your couch, and this is your response?" I give my sister the stink-eye.

"Hey. You're the one who's been bitching and moaning about getting out of the house. And I know how much you like music…" Tracy grins.

I jab my finger toward the stage, cringing as the duo onstage hits one wrong note after another. "This is *not* music. This is where music comes to die."

Tracy rolls her eyes. "Quit your whining."

"You did this on purpose."

"Did what?" She gives me the innocent look that lets me know I'm right.

"Brought me to this godforsaken place so I'd quit bitching about being cooped up inside."

She flutters her lashes. "Did I?"

"I hate you so much right now."

Another grin stretches across her face, and she leans forward, ruffling my hair. "No, you don't. Besides. Not much you can do about it." She stands up and heads for the bar.

Dammit. I hate the fact that my sister is right. Almost as much as I hate the fact that I'm at the mercy of her and my brother-in-law for the foreseeable future.

Shit.

My leg throbs, almost as if echoing my dismay, and I wedge one of my crutches under my cast in an attempt to get it elevated in a semi-comfortable position.

Unfortunately, I don't know that there is such a thing.

I shoot my leg a disgusted look. Another two weeks of this monstrosity. Then at least another four in a shorter cast and probably a walking boot after. Out of commission for the rest of the year. Shoot me now.

Although, I guess I should be thankful that at least I'm able to be up and around. Unlike the previous three weeks, where I was pretty much relegated to my sister and brother-in-law's guest bed or couch with my leg elevated to control the pain and swelling.

But seriously. I'm liable to be batshit crazy by the time I'm fully healed.

Assuming I do, in fact, fully heal.

I do my best to squash the little voice of uncertainty that reminds me I'm not young anymore. That this time, my injury might not heal up quite so fast. Or at all.

Broken bones pretty much come with the territory in my line of work. But it's a hell of a lot easier to heal when you're in your teens and early twenties. Not quite as easy when you're twenty-eight and already full of hardware.

I've known a couple of guys who sustained similar injuries. They're not on tour anymore.

Fuck.

The queasy mixture of fear and uncertainty rolls through my gut once again.

What the hell am I gonna do if my leg doesn't heal like it's supposed to? Not like my years of BMX and Motocross racing have prepared me for any real-world jobs. Unless there's a job market for semi-decent has-beens somewhere I don't know about.

"We don't need no stinking men!"

The shout from the stage area jars me from my thoughts.

While I feel honor-bound to maintain my air of disgust at my sister's choice in bars, I have to admit that it's not that bad. It seems like everyone's having a good time, and for a karaoke place, there's a pretty decent crowd. In fact, if I weren't throwing myself such a pity party, I'd probably get up there myself.

My eyes track the duo as they head back to their seats. Actually, the shorter one's pretty damned cute. Chin-length blonde hair, skin that flushes as she darts me a green-eyed glance, and a nice ass that holds my attention as she steers the taller woman past me toward the bar.

Something niggles at the back of my brain as she takes a seat. Why does that other woman they're sitting with look familiar?

"Megan!" my sister calls out. She takes the beers from the bartender, then heads toward the familiar-looking woman.

Megan. That's right. Shit. How bad does my luck have to be for my sister to know one of my one-night stands? And to run into her again when I can't make a quick getaway?

If I'm lucky, she won't remember me. Or at least that I snuck out in the middle of the night after I'd sobered up. Although judging by the clenching of her jaw when Tracy points my way, I'm pretty sure she does.

I give her a weak smile, nodding my head in acknowledgement.

Megan sends me a death-glare before turning back to Tracy. The taller of the blondes gives me a shrewd look, while the shorter blonde makes eye contact again before her gaze skitters away. I can see her blush deepening from here.

And then I can't. Because Tracy's blocking my view.

She sets a bottle in front of me, then settles into her seat. "So." She sips her beer, then tilts her head and studies me.

I grip my bottle, bracing for yet another lecture.

"Any chance you're looking for a job?"

My hand pauses mid-way to my mouth. "What?" I set my bottle back on the table.

She nods toward the section of bar where the three women are engaged in what appears to be a heated discussion. "It just so happens that Kylie and Lauren own a bicycle shop. And they recently lost their mechanic."

"Huh."

"Yeah."

I've been around bikes my whole life. Hell. They *are* my life.

Tracy eyes my cast. "I have no idea if your leg's up for it, but you definitely have the skills. And I think you'd be really good at it."

"Thanks." Despite all her lectures, my sister has actually been one of my biggest champions. And she's right—I *do* have the skills. I've been working on bikes for as long as I can remember. First bicycles, then motorcycles. A combination of intrigue and hope pushes at the edges of my misgivings. "Wait." I narrow my eyes. "Is this some of your reverse psychology stuff? Like, you really want me to stay on your couch for another couple of months?" My sister's always been the smart one. And now she actually *is* a psychologist.

She snorts. "God, no. I don't want you moping around the house."

I scoff. "I am *not* moping."

Tracy gives me one of her pointed looks. "Yeah. You are."

"Hey, you try breaking your leg in three places and see how much fun you are."

She rolls her eyes. "That's not what I mean, and you know it. I just mean you get all antsy when you're cooped up too long. And don't take this the wrong way, but I have enough antsiness with Reece. I don't know how much more our house can handle."

I crack a smile at the mention of my four-year-old nephew. She's right—she and Craig have their hands full with him. He's a smart little chatterbox with a seemingly endless source of energy. I've loved getting to spend more time with him, but I have no idea how they manage to keep up with him.

"Seriously." She nudges my good leg with her foot. "I think this might be a nice fit for you. You should at least check it out."

"Thanks. Good to know my older sister's still looking out for me."

She shrugs. "Well, someone's got to."

I ignore her implication that I don't look after myself, cutting a glance back toward the women's table. "Who works there?"

"The two sisters, Kylie and Lauren."

Huh. No Megan. "And that's it? The other one doesn't work there?"

Tracy laughs. "Megan? In a bike store. Noooo." I relax a bit as Tracy continues. "And apparently, their uncle works there part-time, but he's having surgery. Or had surgery. I don't know. Kylie was kind of all over the place. So?" She raises her eyebrows. "What do you think?"

I take a pull on my beer as my gaze slides back toward the table of hotties.

The shorter cutie catches my eye again, and I can feel the familiar revving of my engine. Something I haven't felt since my injury.

I think that as long as Megan doesn't have revenge on her mind, and assuming my leg's up for it, this could be a very nice diversion indeed.

CHAPTER THREE

Lauren

"Seriously?" I hiss-whisper, my gaze sliding back to Jake and Tracy. "You cannot just offer a job to a stranger." Particularly when said stranger is so damned hot.

Megan nods. "Agreed. Especially to *him*."

Kylie looks back at their table. "Why not? What's wrong with him?"

"You mean besides the fact that he has a gigantic cast?" I ask.

"It's not like he'll be using his feet to repair the bikes." Kylie shrugs and swings her gaze to Megan. "Besides, your friend Tracy seems to think he'd be good at it, in spite of the bum leg. And even if he can only give us a few hours a day, that's still better than what we have now."

Megan growls, and her face contorts like she's fighting with herself. "She's not really my friend. I know Tracy from spin class." Her shoulders drop with her sigh. "You remember that guy I told you about? That kind-of-sort-of-famous one from a couple years back?"

I give her a blank look. Honestly, Megan goes through so many men that I stopped paying attention to the details a long time ago.

"Well, that's him," she continues. "And apparently, he's Tracy's brother."

"Really?" Kylie's head swivels back to their table. "Sort-of-famous how?"

"Some kind of biker—bicycles? Motorcycles?" Megan's auburn curls bounce as she shakes her head. "I don't really remember. Just that he was a big enough name to be on tour and to have sponsors."

"Wow." Kylie nods. "Now I really hope he can work. Might increase business if people knew we had a pro at the shop."

"Well, if he's there," Megan says, "then I definitely won't be."

"You never come by anyway," I reply.

"Yeah," Kylie adds. "Besides. I would've thought you'd be scrambling all over yourself to have another hookup with him."

Megan sniffs. "Well. I make it a point not to chase guys who up and leave in the middle of the night without so much as a goodbye."

Oh. He's *that* type of guy. Should've known.

Jake catches me looking at him, and something that feels a lot like lust jolts through my system.

Damn. Even if he's as much of a player as Megan is, he's still ridiculously hot. But who am I kidding? Not like someone like him would ever find someone like me attractive. I'm not even sure I'll be able to speak when he's in close proximity. And if I do, no doubt it'll be something embarrassing.

Because I may be many things—smart, level-headed, reliable. But smooth around hot guys is definitely not one of them.

"Maybe we can see if Uncle Pete can delay his surgery," I say. "Just until we can find someone else."

Kylie's knuckles tighten around her glass, and her expression hardens. "No. We don't need Uncle Pete to bail us out. We can do this."

I know enough about Kylie's stubborn streak to know not to try to push the issue. Add in her blood alcohol level and I really don't stand a chance. Not to mention the fact that Aunt Sheila already rearranged her work schedule for Uncle Pete's surgery. Besides, Kylie's right. We *can* do this. Well, the business part, anyway. The talking to hot guys part, not so much.

Which makes the fact that Jake and his sister are coming this way extremely inconvenient. I glance around, considering making a run for it, and spy Megan hightailing it to the far side of the bar.

Traitor.

Thank God Kylie's still here. Although given the number of drinks she's had so far, I'm not entirely sure that's a good thing. Especially since she seems to be hell-bent on giving this guy a job. She flashes Jake one of her killer smiles. "So?" Kylie asks, after a round of introductions. "Did your sister tell you about our little problem?"

Jake's eyes dart to where Megan's flirting with Andrew.

The previous lust dissipates into a mixture of resignation and disappointment. Damn. If Megan and

Jake wind up having an encore, will that make things *more* or *less* awkward?

"Yes," Jake says. "And I have to say, I'm intrigued."

The deep timbre of his voice sends those little shivers racing down my spine.

The shivers hit yet again as my focus shifts to him, meeting some of the most gorgeous eyes I've ever seen—long lashes ring his chocolatey gaze, and the crescent moon of a scar below the corner of one eye just adds to that air of danger.

Megan has hooked up with some hot guys since I've known her, but I've never been this attracted to them.

Double damn.

I blink, then give my head a quick shake as if trying to break the hypnotic pull of his gaze. Come on, Lauren. Get your head in the game. Kylie may sound like her normal self, but she *did* just get her heart stomped on. Not to mention the fact that her blood alcohol level is probably higher than mine.

Kylie smirks at me, then points to Jake's cast. "Are you planning to work with your feet?"

Confusion clouds his features. "Uh, no?"

"Good." Kylie gives me a triumphant smile, then turns back to him. "Your sister said you're good with bikes. What do you do?"

Jake's forearms flex as he tightens his grip on his crutches. "Racing. Started with BMX bikes when I was young. Then moved on to Motocross."

Her eyes narrow, and she nods toward his injured leg. "What happened?"

He wrinkles his nose as if in disgust. "Training accident. Hit a roller wrong, got thrown off-balance. Broke my ankle and higher up on my leg."

"He's doing much better," Tracy chimes in. "And I swear, he's a fabulous mechanic."

I clear my throat. "Do you have references?" I eke out.

Good. Yeah. That was a totally legit question. Except for some reason that makes the corner of his mouth lift. Which sends those excited shivers racing through me once more.

Oh, for Uncle Pete's sake.

"Yeah," Jake says. "I can probably pull something together for you if you want it."

"Yes." I nod. "I want you." My eyes widen. "*It*. I want *it*." Crap. Not helping yourself here, Lauren. "Not *It*. Or that. Your references. Nothing else."

Oh, my God. Shut up already.

Jake's eyebrow ticks upward, an amused gleam lighting his eyes.

Kylie shoots me a questioning look before turning back to Jake. "Right. Anyway... Why don't you come by tomorrow, see if you think it's something you can handle? We open at nine."

Jake shifts on his crutches, his eyes downcast as if studying his leg. Lifting his head, he gives first Kylie, then me, a confident smile. "Yeah. I think I can handle it."

Great. Hottie Jake hanging out in the bike shop for several hours a day.

He might be able to handle it.

But the question is, can I?

CHAPTER FOUR

Jake

Tracy opens the car door and extracts my crutches. "You sure you don't want a pillow?"

I give her a dirty look as I begin the awkward task of getting out of her back seat. "No, Mom. I think I'll pass on taking a pillow with me on my first day at a new job."

She lightly cuffs me on the back of my head as I perch on the edge of the seat to slide my backpack on. "Shut up. I'm just trying to help."

"I know." Taking the crutches from her, I haul myself upright and tuck them under my armpits. "And seriously. Thank you. For everything." I wink. "And if it'll make you feel any better, you will be the first person I call if I have a pillow emergency."

She rolls her eyes, but the worry lines fade as a smile tugs at her mouth. "Yeah, yeah. Just be sure to take it easy, okay?"

"Yeah, yeah," I echo, maneuvering to avoid another swat. With a grin, I shoo her away. "Now go on. Get out of here. You're driving me crazy."

A sigh equal parts resignation and exasperation accompanies her head shake. "Fine." Amusement dances in her eyes. "Love you, Jerk."

Ugh. She knows how much I hate saying the L word. How it makes me twitchy and uncomfortable, even around those I actually *do* love. And, of course, she used my old nickname. The one she'd taken delight in when she'd realized how close jerk and Jake actually are.

I raise my middle finger in answer.

Cackling, she opens her car door, hesitating before climbing back inside. "See you later. And seriously, don't hesitate to text me or Craig when you need a ride."

"Please. Like you won't be checking in every hour."

Tracy's eyes dart away.

"Uh-huh. That's what I thought. Now seriously. Go. I'll be fine."

She presses her lips together. "I just worry about you."

"Yeah, I know." For as big of a cheerleader as she is, I also know how much my reckless lifestyle keeps her up at night. How much she wishes I'd just settle down and "get a real job." One that doesn't put me at risk of ending up in the hospital every day.

Just like I know how to make those worry lines disappear. In my best falsetto, I belt out the chorus of Gloria Gaynor's *I Will Survive,* pointing at the exit to the parking lot as I tell her she's not welcome anymore.

As expected, Tracy's frown disappears, and she rolls her eyes again, this time with a hint of a smile on her face. "Alright, alright. I'm going. See you later, Jerk."

I grin, ignoring the curious stares of the passersby who were privy to my impromptu concert, then crutch up the street.

I have to hand it to Tracy and Craig. They picked a decent place to settle down. A college town with a diverse population, a ton of hiking and biking trails, nearby mountains and lakes. Not that the college part appeals to me. Books and I have never been great friends. And right now, the activities aren't all that appealing either. Well, they are. But I can't really do any of them. Not with a busted leg.

And it's not like I'm actually looking to settle down, despite Tracy's nagging. But if I were, I could probably see myself in some place like this.

I'm just not ready for it to be anytime soon.

The churning in my gut slows as I reach the bike shop—Bike Moore. Kind of cheesy, but I like it. People *should* bike more.

I pause outside the door and catch my breath. Damn. Speaking of people being more active… I really hope I didn't oversell my ability. I can do the work, no problem, but hauling this big-ass cast around is definitely a workout.

Shit. I probably should've taken Tracy up on her pillow suggestion. I hate it when she's right.

With an exasperated sigh, I shove aside my doubts. After all, this is just a trial run. Not like it's an actual job that matters.

Except, it kind of does.

The more I thought about it last night, the more I liked the idea of getting out of Tracy and Craig's house. Getting off my ass and out of my head. Doing something to fill the yawning void of who-knows-how-much-longer until I can get back out on tour. Because that's something else she's right about. I *am* getting mopey. And antsy.

Not to mention the fact that I hate being a sponge.

I know people see me and think "slacker," but I'm actually very driven. And that's something else that scares me. Because while I've poured my heart and soul into the racing world, I've never been able to crack into the top tiers. I've always done well enough to keep myself afloat, but not well enough to build any kind of decent nest egg.

And it's not like I'm getting any younger.

So, add my current medical expenses to my loss of income from not racing, and this job might actually matter more than even *I* want to admit.

Tamping down the nerves usually reserved for a big event, I plaster a smile on my face, prop the door open with a crutch, and shuffle through. The store isn't huge, but it looks like they have a good selection. A few high-end bikes in the display windows, several rows of bicycles running along one side and the back wall, clothing and equipment along another wall and scattered among various display racks.

A raised male voice from the side of the room draws my attention. Glancing over, I see Lauren behind the counter, a pained expression on her flushed face as she talks to what I'm guessing is a customer. A rather pissed customer, by the sound of it.

Relief washes over her face when she sees me standing in the doorway. "Here's one of our mechanics. We'll be happy to take a look at that for you. On the house."

The man turns to face me, his eyebrows furrowing. "Who are you?"

"Jake." I nod to the bike at his side. "What's the issue?"

He rakes his gaze over me, then narrows his eyes. "The *issue* is that I paid to get my brakes fixed, but now the shifter's not working. And I'm *supposed* to go biking with my son this afternoon. It's our day together."

Lauren's gaze darts to mine, the question clear in her eyes.

I give her a slight nod, then turn my attention back to the customer. "I'm free now. I'll be happy to take a look."

The man purses his lips, then exhales a sigh. "Okay. I have a couple of other errands to run, and then I'll stop back. But if you guys screw it up again…"

"Don't worry. I've got this." I flash him my most confident smile, waiting until the door closes behind him before letting out a low whistle. "Wow. No pressure, right?"

"Huh?"

"First day, angry customer. Guess I'd better know what I'm doing."

Her eyes round into saucers. "You do, right? Know what you're doing?"

"With these?" I wave my hand, gesturing toward the bike next to the counter. "Yes. With my life in general? Not so much." Crap. How'd that last part slip out?

A faint smile graces her lips, and the tension in her shoulders melts just a bit. "Good." Her green eyes widen again. "Not good that you don't know what you're doing with your life, I mean good that you can fix bikes."

Damn. She *is* cute. Especially when she's flustered. The flush highlights her cheekbones, and her bottom lip looks even more luscious after she's been working it with her teeth.

Focus, Jake. And not on her mouth. I shift on my crutches and nod toward the bike. "So, uh, you think you could give me a hand?"

A nervous laugh bubbles out of her. "Believe me. You do *not* want me near that thing. I am strictly the numbers side of the business. And sometimes customer service, too, when Kylie's not around."

I glance down at my leg and pull a face. "I kind of need some help getting the bike to wherever it is I'll be working on it. And probably some help getting it up onto the stand."

"Oh. Yeah. That I can handle." She walks the bike toward the back of the shop, and I follow. Despite my best intentions, my eyes keep straying to her ass. And the way it fills out her jeans. And dammit, if I'm not careful, there's gonna be something obvious about what's going on in *my* pants.

Come on, dude. Focus. And not on her ass. Focus on your own walking. 'Cause nothing says "I got this" quite like stumbling over your crutches and face-planting in front of your new boss.

It's almost a relief when she opens a door in the back, revealing the workshop area. The good thing is that I'm no longer ogling her backside. But that's only because I'm busy inspecting the room. It's a mess. Despite adequate shelving and storage, tools are strewn across the work surfaces, and it looks like a couple of projects have been abandoned. A partially stripped bike is up on a repair stand, while another bike rests against a side table.

"Do these need work, too?" I jut my chin toward the bikes in question.

Lauren nods. "I think so. But they're ours, so they're lower on the priority list."

"Your personal bikes?"

"No. We have about a dozen that we rent out. There's usually a couple that need work, but I have no idea what AJ was doing to them." She winces in apology. "Sorry."

I give her a reassuring smile. "No problem. I'm sure I'll figure it out. If there's one thing I'm good at, it's bikes."

And women.

But it's probably best not to overshare on the first day.

CHAPTER FIVE

Lauren

After helping Jake get the disgruntled customer's bike into position on the stand, I hightail it to the front of the store.

Where the hell is Kylie?

I mean, I know theoretically where she is. She's at City Hall, in a meeting about the new city-wide bike program. And it's probably a good thing, too. She seemed a bit calmer this morning, but still. Every time she glanced toward the back of the store, it looked like she was trying to set it on fire with her mind.

So, while it's likely in all of our best interests to have her out on some errands for a while, it leaves me here in the shop with Jake. Hot Jake. Hot Jake with his tattooed arms, warm chocolate eyes, and easy smile.

Hot Jake who is so far off limits it's not even funny.

Even if I thought I stood some sort of chance at catching the eye of a guy like that, there's no way I'd ever do something with an employee. Even though Kylie did. Or maybe *especially* since Kylie did.

Good thing Dad wasn't here to see what was going on at the family business.

The familiar pinch in my chest returns.

It's been six months, and it still feels like it's Dad's business. Like he could walk through the door at any minute. I know it hasn't been all that long, but when is it gonna get easier?

Of course, it probably doesn't help that I'm spending more time at the shop than I have since I was a teenager. That his shop is now partially mine.

The shop I never really wanted in the first place.

Sure, he always talked about leaving it to us, but we never expected it to be this soon. And I never really expected to do anything with it. But after a few weeks of trying to do it on her own, Kylie asked for help, and what was I supposed to do? Let her keep floundering? Of course not. That's not what family does.

Doesn't mean there aren't days I wonder if I made the right choice, though.

Swallowing against the lump of emotions in my throat, I take a deep breath. Focus, Lauren. There's too much to do to let yourself fall apart now.

There were many times growing up that I resented being the level-headed "smart" sister. Now, however, I'm grateful. Because there is nothing I find quite so reassuring as checking things off my to-do list.

After refiling yet another stack of paperwork and balancing our bank account, I feel marginally better. At least about my organizational skills.

Jake, not so much.

My finger hovers over the keyboard, itching to do yet another search on our newest employee.

Not that I expect to find anything more than what I found last night, which was sparse at best. Mostly Google hits about his rankings and racing career, with a few more recent trade articles noting his injury and questioning his future. And while the dearth of dirt on him was more than a little disappointing, at least I now have a working knowledge of what he does for a living. And that the rollers that caused his injury are those little groups of hills on the race course. And that those daredevils are actually pretty good athletes. Who look seriously hot in their racing uniforms.

Good thing Jake's just wearing regular clothes these days.

My throat goes dry at the mental picture of how his T-shirt stretched across his chest. I'll bet he looks even better with his shirt off.

The buzz of my cell phone jars me from my thoughts of the hot guy in the back room.

Damn.

Seeing Aunt Sheila's name, my gut clenches as I answer. "Hey. Everything okay?"

"Yeah," Sheila says. "He's out of surgery. Doctor says it went well."

I exhale a breath of relief. "Good. How're you holding up?"

"So far so good. Of course, ask me after the first week. One of us is liable to be insane by that point."

"Well, you know he's always welcome here at the shop." My eyes dart to the back. "Which reminds me, I should probably fill you in on a few things."

"Oh, honey," Aunt Sheila says after I give her a rundown of the happenings of the last twenty-four hours. "Why didn't you say something? We could've postponed Pete's surgery."

"Yeah. I know. But you shouldn't have to." They've done so much for us since Dad died. They need to take some time to take care of themselves.

"You know it's no problem. That's what family's for."

"Thanks, Aunt Sheila, but we'll manage. Let us know what we can do."

"Just let him hang out at the shop when he starts getting ornery."

I chuckle. "Will do."

After we hang up, I work through a couple of online orders before my thoughts start to stray to the back of the shop again. I'm not sure if it's a good thing or a bad thing that I haven't heard a peep out of the back room. I guess it either means that Jake has been as absorbed in his work as I've been in mine, or that he's already snuck out the back, much like he did to Megan. Although in the world of possible bad scenarios, it's much more probable that he would've fallen.

Crap. What if he injures himself even more? I should probably double-check our workers' comp policy.

I powerwalk to the back, letting out a breath when I see him seated on a stool, his eyes closed as he slowly turns the bike pedal.

The pinch in my chest relaxes, replaced instead by a warm, pleasant sensation. Almost like my hormones let out a collective sigh.

As if sensing my presence, Jake opens his eyes. "Hey. You're just in time. This sucker is smooth as silk now. Just want to check a few other things and then I think it's done."

I nod, my thoughts momentarily stalled by the smile he unleashes. "Great... Uh... Thanks." Come on, Lauren. Stop drooling. Focusing on the bike instead of his mesmerizing features, I ask, "So, AJ didn't mess anything up too badly?"

"Nah. Just had to tighten up the cables and readjust the derailleur limits. Piece of cake."

"Oh. Good. I like cake."

Laughter dances in his eyes. "Good to know."

I can feel the heat gathering in my face as he studies me, my brain clunking like it can't quite get itself in gear. Cake, Lauren? Seriously? "I mean, don't get me wrong. I like pie, too. I'm an equal opportunity dessert enthusiast."

Oh, my God. Shut up.

"She's not lying." Kylie's appearance in the doorway makes me jump. "She once tried to stab me with a fork over a hot fudge brownie sundae."

While I should probably be glad that my sister's appearance means I'm no longer one-on-one with Jake, I'm not so sure it won't just lead to more humiliation.

Despite the glare I aim in her direction, she shrugs. "What? I'm just warning the poor guy."

"I appreciate it." His lips twitch as he points at his leg. "I'm already down one limb. Can't afford to lose any others."

Kylie's gaze bounces around the room, and she shifts from one foot to the other. "You, uh, need anything?"

Jake shakes his head. "Not quite yet."

"Great." She catches my eye and nods toward the front of the shop. "Can I borrow you?"

"Absolutely." Kylie disappears out of sight, and I flash Jake a smile. "Let me know when you need a hand job."

I can feel the fire on my cheeks as the words play over again in my head.

Oh. My. God.

"I mean, when you need a hand. Or when you're finished with the job. Not when you, you know, need a hand job. Because I am *definitely* not offering that."

"Um… Okay."

I catch the mixture of amused interest sparkling in Jake's eyes before I turn tail to follow Kylie.

Holy hell. What is wrong with me?

I mean, I know what's wrong with me. Good-looking guys make me nervous. Always have. But seriously. I'm a grown woman! And a business owner. And this guy is my employee.

Shit. Am I gonna have to file a sexual harassment suit against *myself*?

"So…" Kylie leans against the counter, her lips pursed. "Jake—yes or no?"

I really want to say no. After all, I clearly can't handle being around him. Not without making a total idiot out of myself, anyway. And how wise is it really to hire a stranger we met at a karaoke bar? Although it's not like he's a total stranger. Megan knows his sister. And him. Biblically.

I wonder again about the wisdom of hiring someone who snuck out on my friend. Although, if we restricted our candidates to people Megan hasn't hooked up with, we'd be working with a very limited pool.

Besides, the references he sent last night checked out. And he does seem to know what he's doing bike-wise. Plus, it doesn't really seem fair not to give him a chance just because he slept with one of my friends. Or because he's attractive and makes my brain go squishy. While wholly inconvenient for me, that seems petty, not to mention kind of like reverse discrimination.

If all else fails, I can probably just avoid him. And never, ever open my mouth when he's around.

Plastering a smile on my face, I nod. "Yes."

Relief washes across Kylie's features. "Oh, thank God."

"But only part-time. You know we can't afford more."

"Yet." Kylie pushes a packet of papers toward me. "If we win this bid, there's a $15,000 grant up front, plus the monthly stipend."

Hope takes root as I thumb through the details. "Wow. That's even better than I thought. What do you think our chances are?"

Kylie shrugs. "I don't know. I mean, we're a third-generation business. You'd think that would carry some sway in the community. But Spencer's chummy with a couple of the council members."

I'm not sure if her disgusted lip curl is due to the fact that she hates playing politics as much as I do or because of the mention of her high-school-boyfriend-turned-competition. Probably a combination of the two.

"Well, maybe he'd be willing to help us out."

She gives me one of her laser death glares, and I barely refrain from rolling my eyes. Despite the fact that Kylie hates Spencer's guts, I actually kind of like the guy. Much better than any of her other boyfriends, that's for sure.

"We don't need his help. Besides, he'd probably give us wrong information in order to secure the bid for himself."

It's on the tip of my tongue to argue that I really don't think Spencer would do that, but I swallow my words. Because one—Kylie's in fighting mode right now, and I stand absolutely no chance of making her see reason. And two—no matter how many times I tell her that I really don't think Spencer's out to get us, she's still hung up on whatever happened between them eons ago.

Flipping through the mail on the counter, Kylie flinches, her expression sliding from one of irritation to one of discomfort. "Crap."

"What?"

"Pedals & Medals." She fingers a brochure, then sets it on the counter.

I open it up and peruse it, double-checking our ad. Bike Moore has been a sponsor of the event since it started, and for several years, the shop has had a booth on-site for added exposure. "What about it?"

"I'm not sure I can do it."

"What do you mean? We're already sponsoring it." I hold up the brochure. "We already paid."

"Yeah. I know. I just…" She swallows. "I'm not sure I can handle the booth."

"But… You love working the booth. You always do it." It's one of the things I admire most about Kylie—her ability to schmooze and talk to strangers. Just like Dad. Something I definitely did *not* inherit.

"Yeah. With Dad." Kylie gives me what I presume to be a pleading smile, but comes closer to being a wince. "Please? Could you do it this year?" She blinks, her eyes shiny. "I'll owe you."

Crap. There's a reason I try to stick to the behind-the-scenes stuff. I hate these types of things. But I also don't want Kylie breaking down in the middle of the event. "I don't know…"

"Hey, sorry to interrupt." Jake flashes an apologetic smile as Kylie and I turn toward him. "Can I get a hand?" Jake's eyes dart to mine, and it's clear he's still amused by my faux pas. "The bike's done."

"Absolutely." Kylie's eyes widen, and I can see the moment inspiration strikes. It coincides with the sinking sensation in my gut.

"Any chance you'd like to keep Lauren company Saturday? We have a booth at a big community event. Of course, you'll get paid for your time."

"Uh, sure?"

Kylie turns back to me. "What do you say? Can you man the booth with Jake while I keep an eye on things here?"

Dammit. She is *so* gonna owe me. I sigh. "Fine."

"Thank you," she says, including us both in her grateful smile.

"No problem," Jake replies.

Maybe not for him. But I'm pretty sure my problems are only just beginning.

CHAPTER SIX

Jake

Dammit. I probably should've listened to Tracy. I could really use a pillow right about now.

The first couple of hours weren't bad, but the ache in my leg has been steadily increasing, and if I don't get it elevated again soon, I'm pretty sure I'm gonna regret it.

Scanning the room, I take stock of the options. A couple of boxes that I'm not sure would hold my weight. Metal cabinets that I don't think I'd be able to move even if I was in one piece. And built-in counters that run the length of two walls.

Shit. I should've asked for help when Lauren and Kylie were back here earlier. It's bad enough that I needed help getting the bike on and off the stand. I don't know that I want to keep drawing attention to the fact that they'd probably be better off hiring someone else.

But I also don't want to mess my leg up any worse.

As much as I enjoy taking risks, doing anything that might screw up my healing would be nothing short of idiotic. Not that I haven't been called that on more than several occasions. By more than a few people.

The mixture of anger and self-loathing punches me in the chest.

Joking jabs by my sister and friends are one thing, but the echoes of voices from my youth still get to me. Add in the voices of doubt about my future, and…

Focus, Jake!

I take a deep breath, trying to redirect my thoughts. No sense going down that road. You're here. You're fine. Except for the fact that you're sitting on a perfectly good stool while your leg's still throbbing.

Idiot.

Giving myself a mental eye roll, I swallow a couple ibuprofens from the bottle in my backpack, then carefully slide to the floor and wrestle the heel of my cast onto the rung of the stool, high enough to get my leg elevated above my heart without risking a pulled hamstring to boot.

A relieved sigh escapes as the throbbing subsides. I don't know that I've ever been so happy to be lying on a cold concrete floor in my life.

While I'm still disgusted that I have to take breaks like this, at least they're becoming less frequent. Nor do I need the heavy-duty pain meds any more. And I did manage to fix that customer's bike without having to stop. So, all in all, I guess things are heading in the right direction. But still. The end point of that direction is a long way off.

My chest constricts again, but I refocus on the positives. I'm healing. I'm getting to spend a lot of time with my nephew. And there are worse places I could be hanging out during my recuperation than a bike shop. With things to fix. And good-looking women.

While I tend not to be super-choosy when it comes to my type, I have to admit that well-rounded blondes sit near the top of my wish list. Especially entertaining, well-rounded blondes.

Because Lauren is nothing if not entertaining.

I'd almost burst out laughing when she accidentally offered me a hand job. But I could tell she was horrified. And while I wasn't offended and definitely would've said something flirty if I knew her better, making someone feel bad about themselves when they're already clearly embarrassed hits a little too close to home for me. Doesn't mean I can't entertain the *idea*, however…

My thoughts wander back to the possibilities of Lauren's hands on me.

Shit.

This would probably be much easier if I were working with a bunch of dudes. At least then I wouldn't have to be worried about getting boners at my place of employment.

"Oh, my God!"

The distressed cry startles me, and my eyelids snap open.

Lauren's standing in the doorway, eyes like saucers, one hand covering her mouth while the other holds the handle of a bicycle.

Great. Now she's gonna think I've been sleeping on the job. Or worse. "It's not what it looks like." I glance down at my shorts, relieved to see that my leg is the only thing raised right now.

Her shoulders relax, and relief replaces the concern on her face as she lets out a breath. "I thought you fell."

"Nope. Just elevating my leg." Definitely *not* thinking about my boss. Or what her hands could do. I give her a sheepish smile and struggle to sit up. The smile falters as I try to figure out how to get back to my feet again. Shit. Probably should've thought things through a little more.

Story of my life.

"Well, uh, okay," Lauren says. "I'll just leave you to it, then."

"Wait." I really hate that I even have to ask, but if I don't, no telling how much longer I'll be stuck down here. "Could you, uh, help me up?"

Her eyes widen again, and her cheeks flush. "Oh. Yeah. Sorry."

"Don't be. It's my own stupid fault." Planting my good leg, I hold out my hands.

The stain on her cheeks intensifies, and her eyes fly to my hands.

Oh. Right. They're probably covered in grease. With another wince-smile, I wipe them on my pants. "Sorry.

"Don't be." She exhales and shakes her head, then offers her hands. Bracing herself, she nods. "On the count of three, okay?"

"Yep."

"One...Two...Three."

She tugs me upright, and my hands tighten around hers as I fight to keep my balance.

Her hands are soft, and from this distance, I get a whiff of vanilla that I'm guessing is either her shampoo or body lotion.

Oh, damn.

As if I needed to add more awkwardness to the situation, I can feel my groin tightening. Again.

Seriously?

If this keeps up, there's a good chance she won't be the only one embarrassing herself.

"Thanks." I flash her a smile and let go. "I'm good."

"Yeah." Her gaze lingers on my lips for a few beats before she shakes her head as if to clear it. "Oh. No problem." Her eyebrows furrow as I get settled on my crutches. "How'd you get down there anyway?" she asks.

"Gravity?"

A hesitant smile curves Lauren's lips. "Ha-ha. Very funny."

"I thought so." I return her smile, then nod toward the bike leaning against the doorway. Focus, Jake. "So, did you bring me another present?"

"What? Oh. Yeah. Nothing big. Just an annual tune-up." She glances at my leg. "But no rush. It can wait."

"Nah. I'm fine." Probably best to keep myself occupied anyway. I point to the bike stand. "If you can help me get that bike off and this one on, I can get started on it." We change out the bikes before I speak again. "So, uh, you want to fill me in on what I signed up for?"

"Huh?" Lauren's brow knits in confusion.

"This weekend? With you?"

"Oh. *That.* You don't really have to go."

"Why not? Don't you want me to go?"

Her cheeks pinken. "No. I mean, yes. I mean, *I* don't really want to go."

"Why not?" I ask again.

Her lower lip disappears between her teeth, and her eyes dart to me before they skitter away again.

An idea races through my head. One I don't like. Because I'm getting the feeling here that despite what she said, it might actually be one of the rare cases where "It's not you, it's me" is a total lie, and that it might actually be me. Which is weird, because I could've sworn that I was detecting some interest from her side.

Crap.

Maybe that's not what the lip biting and blushing was about after all, and my intuition is as screwed up as my leg.

"It's just…" Lauren rolls her bottom lip between her teeth again, then winces. "I'm not all that great at being the public face of the company. That's really Kylie's cup of tea."

Relief washes through me. "Oh. Well, then. No problem."

"Why not?"

"Because I do public stuff all the time." Or used to, anyway. I smack away the doubts and continue. "Sure, most of the Motocross gig's racing, but part of it's PR stuff, too. Autographs, talking with sponsors, that kind of thing."

"Oh."

"So as long as you can handle the business-y side of the conversations, I can handle the other stuff."

The previous hesitancy in her eyes disappears. "Like a team."

"Exactly."

She takes her lower lip between her teeth again, and her eyes dart between my mouth and eyes. The blush creeps back onto her cheeks and she blows out a breath, the corners of her lips lifting as she nods. "Okay, then. Go, Team."

"Yeah. Go, Team." While I've never been one for team sports, I am definitely willing to make an exception in this instance.

As long as she doesn't have pom-poms. Or a cheerleader outfit. With a sweater stretching across firm, ripe breasts and a barely-there skirt showing off her legs.

My blood makes a run south of the border, yet again.

Damn.

This has the potential to be the most uncomfortable team meeting ever.

CHAPTER SEVEN

Lauren

Plunking the last box onto our Pedals & Medals table, I begin to unpack.

Banner and tablecloth? Check. Swag for giveaways? Check. An overabundance of nervous energy and a high likelihood that I'll do something cringe-worthy in Jake's presence today? Double check.

I unfold the Bike Moore banner and clip it into place, my sweaty palms making the action a little more complicated than it should be.

Cool it, Lauren. Have some dignity. He's just an employee.

A guy employee.

A hot guy employee.

A hot guy employee with gorgeous eyes and intriguing ink and strong hands that I wouldn't mind holding again.

I blow out a breath, trying not to remember the way his touch sent little jolts of pleasure zipping across my skin. Trying not to imagine his long, calloused fingers wandering higher up my arms and exploring body parts that've seen way too little action recently.

Argh! Why couldn't Jake be balding with a beer belly? It would make my life so much easier right now.

I glance at my watch, and the nervous butterflies in my stomach do the jitterbug once again. He should be here any minute. Although if I'm lucky, maybe he'll be late. Or he won't be able to get a ride.

But then I'd be here in the booth by myself all day.

Crap. I don't know which option would be worse—having Jake here or *not* having Jake here. If only Uncle Pete wasn't still hopped up on pain meds after his surgery, I could have him run interference.

I cast my phone a longing glance. Maybe Sheila could come—

No! Stop it! You are a strong woman. You can do this.

"Am I interrupting something?"

I jump, startled by the seemingly sudden appearance of Jake by my side. How the hell did I not hear his crutches? It's not like he's exactly stealthy. "What? No. Why?"

He gives me a look somewhere between amusement and concern. "Uh, because you were kind of talking to yourself."

Great. Now I'm socially awkward *and* crazy. Might as well start adopting cats right now to complete the picture. "Nope. Just trying to give myself a pep talk."

"Well, then, I guess I showed up just in time. Wouldn't want to miss the team pep talk."

I rack my brain for something that won't make me sound like a lunatic, but all I hear is the excited buzz of my hormones. Jake looks like he hasn't shaved in a day or so, and the Bike Moore T-shirt he's wearing stretches across his chest and shows off his biceps. His forearms flex as he clenches the handles of his crutches, and it's all I can do to keep from reaching out and tracing the intricate lines of his tattoos.

Come on, Lauren. Get a grip.

And *not* on any part of Jake.

What were we talking about? Oh. Right. "Uh... Go, Team?" Instead of the cheerleader-ish arm motion I intended, I find myself doing the jazz hands maneuver.

Ten minutes in and you're already spazzing out. Geez.

Jake shifts on his crutches. "Alright, then. What's the game plan?"

Right. The game plan.

The game plan is to make it through an entire day trying to talk to strangers about my business while in close proximity to someone who makes my IQ drop twenty points.

It's gonna be a really long day.

While I'm glad Jake's here to handle the publicity side of the equation, I'm pretty sure if he wasn't here, I wouldn't have nearly as much foot traffic to worry about. And I'm not altogether sure how many of the women stopping to chat with him will translate into actual Bike Moore customers. I get the feeling that most of them are more interested in getting *his* info, not the business's.

Something that feels a lot like envy courses through my veins as I see yet another woman cooing over him. Throwing back her head and laughing. Running her hand up his tattooed arm.

Damn. She makes flirting look so easy.

And Jake, well, it seems that in addition to bikes, he's pretty adept at the flirting thing himself.

But what did I expect?

I mean, he's a professional athlete and one of the best-looking guys I've ever seen. Flirting's probably like a second language to him.

I stifle a snort. If I could've taken Flirting 101 to satisfy my language arts requirements, I might've considered it. Of course, that probably would've pulled down my GPA, so never mind.

"Hey."

I jump, Jake's hand on my elbow sending a sizzle down my arm.

"Sorry. Didn't mean to startle you."

"What? You didn't startle me." The thudding in my chest argues otherwise.

"Looked like you were in pretty deep thought there for a while."

"Really?" I shake my head and look around the deserted booth. "Why? Did I miss something?"

He gives me a wry smile and eases himself down onto one of the folding chairs. "Nothing of substance." A wince mars his features as he props his cast on one of his crutches. "So... How do you think things are going?"

"Well, you're certainly delivering on that whole being good with strangers thing." Especially the pretty ones.

"What can I say? It's a gift."

The easy grin he gives me makes me feel a bit lightheaded.

Or maybe I'm just dehydrated and hungry. Yeah. Probably that.

Taking advantage of the lull, I sit down, too. "You want a water?" I pull a water bottle and a container of carrot sticks out of the little cooler I brought.

"No, thanks." He gives me a sheepish grin as he pulls his own water out of his backpack. "My sister made sure I came prepared." He holds out a baggie of cookies. "Want one?"

A bubble of laughter rises up and escapes before I can contain it.

Jake gives me a suspicious look. "What? Are you mocking me and my cookies?"

"No." I press my lips together, failing to contain my smile. "It just struck me as funny, that's all. Kind of like we're in grade school and trading lunches."

"Who said anything about trading lunches?" Jake's look turns wary. "I don't want any of your carrot sticks. You keep that healthy stuff to yourself."

"I thought you would be all into the healthy stuff."

His eyebrow rises. "Why's that?"

"Because of the athlete thing." I wave a carrot stick in his general direction. "I don't think that body was built on desserts."

Crap. Way to practically go right ahead and tell him that you're thinking about his body.

One side of Jake's mouth hitches upward, a gleam sparkling in his eye. "Oh, I enjoy desserts just as much as the next guy. Especially the ones with whipped cream and chocolate sauce."

An image of Jake sprawled naked in the bedroom with exactly that pops into my brain. Damn. Is it hot in this tent all of a sudden?

"Hi, Lauren."

I tear my gaze away from Jake, relief sweeping through me at the sight of Spencer standing in front of us. "Spence! Hi!" I'm not sure I've ever been this glad to see one of my sister's exes.

"Just stopped in to see how things are going." Spencer smiles at me, then turns his attention to Jake. "You must be the new guy."

Jake shakes Spencer's hand. "Jake."

Spencer lets out a low whistle. "Hurley said you messed your leg up, but damn, that's a big cast."

"You know Hurley?" Jake asks.

Spencer leans against the table and nods. "Yep. He and I went to school together. I gave him a call when I heard the competition was bringing in a ringer." Spence winks at me, taking the sting out of his words, then turns his attention back to Jake and nods at his leg. "How bad is it?"

Jake's Adam's apple bobs as he swallows. "Bad." His gaze darts to me before returning to

Spence. "Two plates and twelve screws in the ankle and a pin up near my knee."

"Ouch. How long are you out for?" Spence asks.

The muscles in Jake's jaw jump. "Rest of the season, at least."

"Aw, man. That sucks."

Jake huffs a laugh, but the amusement doesn't reach his eyes. "Yeah. Tell me about it."

Spencer looks around the vicinity. "No Kylie this year?"

I shake my head. "No. She, uh, didn't think she was up to it."

A furrow forms between Spencer's eyebrows, concern darkening his expression. "Are you guys doing okay?"

"Yeah. We're fine. Thanks for asking. She just needed a break is all."

Spencer presses his lips together, then nods. "Okay. But Lauren—let me know if you guys need anything."

"Will do. Thanks, Spencer."

"Funny," Jake says, after Spence is out of earshot. "That's not how I pictured the Spawn of Satan."

"What?"

"Your sister may have, ah, told me a little about him."

I roll my eyes. "Don't listen to Kylie. He's a nice guy."

"So, if he's such a nice guy, why does your sister think he's the Devil's spawn?"

"Where do I start?" I munch another carrot stick. "Don't know how much she told you, but he owns one of the other bike shops in town."

"Okay. So, that explains the 'competition' comments."

"Yeah. But that's not the Devil spawn part." I wrinkle my nose. "They used to date."

"Oh."

"Yeah. I still don't know everything that happened between them, but let's just say that Spence has been on Kylie's shit list for well over a decade now."

"Ouch." Jake winces. "That is a *long* time to hold a grudge."

"No kidding."

"Note to self, don't ever get on your sister's bad side."

I bite my lip to try to contain my smile, but it breaks free anyway.

His eyes dip to my mouth, and the queasy giddiness rolls through my stomach again.

Silence stretches between us, and I sift through my brain, trying to find something to fill it. Something preferably not related to his kissable lips or chocolatey eyes.

What were we talking about? Oh, right. "Who's Hurley?"

"One of the guys on the tour."

"How *did* you hurt your leg? Google wasn't all that helpful."

"You Googled me?"

"Uh, yeah. Of course. You know, for employment purposes. Not like, for creepy stalker stuff." I clamp my lips together to try to contain any further threats of awkwardness.

"Ah. Of course." Jake's lips twitch, amusement sparkling in his eyes once again before his expression turns more somber. "Well, thank God I got injured during a training run, otherwise it probably would've been on video. Got too much air under me during a jump, bailed off my bike and landed wrong." He runs a hand through his hair and wrinkles his nose. "Things after that are kind of fuzzy, but I remember the ambulance and then a couple of *super* fun days in the hospital while they tried to put Humpty Dumpty back together again."

"Did it work?"

He shrugs. "We'll see."

The uncertainty in his eyes tugs at my heart. Poor guy. I reach out and lay a hand on his arm, giving it a sympathetic squeeze. "Are you sure you're up to this?" Removing my hand, I wag a finger through the air, indicating the booth.

His expression relaxes. "Definitely. I don't know about you, but I can only stay cooped up for so long. Especially with my sister. Seriously. This job probably kept Tracy and me from killing each other."

"Well then, I'm glad to know our business has been instrumental in preventing fratricide."

He chuckles. "You should put that on the website."

"Bike Moore. Preventing fratricide since 1958."

He laughs again, then sobers. "Is that really how old the shop is?"

"Yep. Our grandfather started it. Then it was our dad's. He died six months ago and left it to Kylie and me." The shop and a lot of financial obligations. The familiar fist of emotion squeezes my throat.

"Sorry to hear that. For what it's worth, I really like your shop."

I give him a shaky smile. "Thanks. I really like you, too." I can feel my eyelids stretch as the horror of my words sink in. Just when we were managing to have a halfway decent conversation, too. "I mean, I think you're doing a really great job. At the shop. As a mechanic."

Jake's lips twitch. "Good to know."

Crap. Where's a crowd of people to talk to when I need one? "Anyway, uh… Keep up the good work."

The corner of Jake's lips rises. "I'll try. Go, Team, right?"

"Yep. Go, Team."

Except *this* part of the team should probably go far, far away. Because I seriously don't know how much more awkward I can be. And I don't want to find out.

CHAPTER EIGHT

Jake

Damn. I don't think I've ever seen anyone move that fast.

I'd been all set to climb to my feet, er, foot, when the elderly couple entered the booth. But Lauren exploded from her seat like she'd been launched from a rocket, and she's been chatting with them ever since.

Guess she really wants to work on her social skills.

Which is just as well, because I am more than happy to sit here and watch. In a strictly professional sort of way, of course. So I can give her feedback. And not just feedback about how much I'd like to entertain some of those dessert fantasies I've been having.

I shift in my seat, the blood making a trip below my imaginary belt once again.

Cool it, Jake. Don't mess anything up. You need this job. And you need to stop wondering what your boss would look like in a whipped cream bikini.

Dammit!

Focus on something else. Something not sexy. Something not related to how cute Lauren is when she's all riled up, her cheeks pink, her green eyes wide and her lips parted like she might—

Argh!

Think unsexy thoughts, think unsexy thoughts…

Tangled bike chains. Which make me think about her hair, tangled. And running my hands through it—

Gah!

Greasy gears. Which are slippery. And dirty. Kinda how I'd like us to be…

My phone pings, and I pull it out of my pocket. Oh, thank God. Saved by Tracy. Nothing less sexy than your sister. "Hey," I say. "You and Reece on your way?"

"Sorry. I was getting him buckled into his car seat to come over, and he started throwing up. Barely made it back into the house before round two started. I don't know how much he's got left in the tank, but so far the eggs we had for breakfast and the hot dogs we had for lunch have made an appearance."

I slap a hand over my mouth, my gag reflex on red alert. "Ugh. Stop." The sounds of someone retching in the background trigger a convulsion of my upper body.

"In the bucket!" Tracy shouts, her voice muffled. "Sorry," she says to me. "I think you're on your own for a ride. And if I were you, I'd steer clear of our house for a little while. Not quite sure how long this is gonna last, and I don't need you adding to the fun."

I've always been a sympathetic puker, a fact my sister knows well. I still don't think she's forgiven me for the time she threw up after having her wisdom teeth taken out, and I wound up ruining the blanket our grandma made for her.

Tamping down another wave of nausea, I tell my sister good luck and hang up. On the bright side, at least I no longer have a raging hard-on. On the not-so-bright side, there's a very real chance I'll wind up blowing chunks in front of Lauren.

Talk about making an impression.

"Everything okay?"

From the look on Lauren's face it's a safe bet I look about as green as I feel.

"Ugh. Give me a minute." I exhale a shaky breath, then fill her in on my conversation with Tracy.

Her nose crinkles, but a smile tips the corners of her mouth.

"What?"

"Sorry. Just wouldn't have taken you for a sympathetic puker. It's kind of nice to see a chink in the armor." Pink tinges her cheeks as she presses her lips together. "So, uh, how old's your nephew?"

"Four."

Her face fills with empathy. "Aw. Poor guy."

"Me or him?"

The smile plays across her lips again. "Him."

"Shoot. And here I was hoping you'd feel sorry enough for me to keep me company while I wait for Pukefest to settle down."

Lauren works her lower lip between her teeth, her brow furrowed as if in deep thought.

Shit. Good job, Jake. Way to make things even more awkward. It's obvious she's trying to figure out a polite way to decline.

"You know what? Forget I asked. It's been a long day, and I'm sure you're ready to get home."

"No. It's not that." She shakes her head and gives me a wry smile. "Okay. It's a little that. But only because my introvert meter is full. Not because I don't want to hang out with you."

"Good. I mean, good that you're okay keeping me company. Not good that your introvert meter's full." Whatever the hell that is. "Anything I can do to help with that?"

She twists her lips to the side. "Not unless you can perform personality transplants."

"Well, you don't want me anywhere near an operating room, what with the whole puking thing. And I definitely don't think you need a personality transplant. But I can probably offer you dinner."

A panicked look crosses her face. "You mean, like a date?"

While I definitely wouldn't mind a date with Lauren, clearly, she doesn't feel the same way about me. "Or, uh, maybe like a bribe? Or a thank you? For saving me from certain death?"

Relief and something that looks like disappointment war on her face. "Oh. Right."

"Plus, we could talk business. I have some ideas I'd like to run past you."

Her mouth rounds into an O, surprise clear on her features.

"Hey. I might not be the smartest guy in the room, but I'm more than just a pretty face."

Her cheeks flush, and she clamps her lips together. Following a few beats of silence, a teasing smile plays on her lips. "Well, to be fair, we're not *in* a room. We're outside."

I grin. "Technicalities…"

"Well then, *technically*, I could really use a burger and a beer to go with the business talk."

"*That* sounds like a wonderful business plan."

But if we wind up ordering dessert, all bets are off.

I adjust my cast on the chair next to me, then settle back while we wait for our food. "So, tell me more about the bike program everyone was talking about."

Lauren stops toying with her silverware, excitement lighting her eyes. "It's this new program the City's putting together. Somebody donated a whole fleet of new bikes, and they're gonna set up little kiosks where you can rent and return them. The City's looking for one of the local bike shops to partner with to get it up and running and then do the maintenance."

"And that's what you guys are bidding on."

"Yep."

"That's cool."

"Yeah, it is. Not only for the city, but for us, too. It would be another revenue stream, plus great exposure."

"Any idea what your chances are?"

Lauren shakes her head. "Nope. But I kind of think Spence has the best shot."

"Why?"

"Because City Council tends to be one of those good ol' boy networks, and in case you couldn't tell, Bike Moore doesn't exactly fit since Dad died. Plus, Spence has the personnel to handle it."

"And you don't?"

Lauren wobbles her head. "Well, technically, we have you and our Uncle Pete. Not that you aren't both great mechanics, but between the two of you, we have three working arms and three good legs, at least for the next few months."

"Hmmm… I can see how that might come across as a bit risky." Our conversation pauses as the waitress distributes our food. "I'm happy to help as long as I can, but I totally get it if you find someone else." Despite the fact that my burger smells delicious, my gut twists at the thought.

Lauren pauses, her French fry mid-ketchup swipe. "Why? Are you leaving?"

"Not yet. Not unless you want me to."

"No. Please. Stay. I really like having you around." Her cheeks pinken. "I mean… You're a really great addition to the shop. You know, because you're good with your hands. As a mechanic." She shoves the fry into her mouth, her eyes skittering away from mine.

While I definitely wouldn't mind showing her what I can do with my hands, *not* as a mechanic, I quash the urge. After all, not only is there that whole boss-employee thing, but I don't want to risk undoing whatever headway we've made today. I have the feeling that if I push too far too fast, she might bolt.

As much as I like seeing her flustered, I also like it when she forgets to be nervous. Because when she calms down enough to hold a decent conversation, she's actually kind of funny. And she definitely has more substance than the women I usually wind up with. They're typically looking for a notch on their bedpost or a check mark in the athlete-slash-famous-person Who-To-Do list. Although if things don't end up working out like I hope, I might not fall into either of those categories anymore.

Tucking my tangled thoughts aside, I refocus on the shop. "So, about those ideas I had earlier…"

Lauren's shoulders relax, relief washing over her features as she takes a bite of her burger. A dot of ketchup clings to the corner of her mouth, and her tongue darts out.

Focus. And not on her lips. Or what you want to do to them.

Lauren raises an eyebrow. "Go ahead."

I cough on the swig of beer I'd been using to try to wash down my lust. Calm down. She did *not* mean to go ahead with kissing her senseless. At least, not right now.

Giving my head a quick shake, I flash her a smile. "Right. My ideas. Well, Reece has been bugging me to come visit the shop."

"Oh. You should totally show him around."

"Okay. I will. But I think others might be interested, too. I got the feeling from several of my conversations today that people would like to watch having their bike repairs done. You know, maybe even like a one-on-one class."

Lauren's mouth makes a downward turn. "Huh. Dad always talked about doing that. Never quite got around to it, though. You'd be willing to do that?"

"Absolutely." Not only do I genuinely like doing stuff like that, it might help me cement my status with the shop for a while.

She takes another bite of her burger, her forehead scrunched in thought while she chews. "Are you any good? At teaching?"

I shrug. "I think so. But maybe just to be sure, you should check me out." Despite the warning bells clanging in my head, I just can't seem to stop myself. And if I'm honest, I don't really want to.

Lauren gulps.

"I mean, you said yourself you're not really good with the bike repair stuff. Maybe you could be like a trial customer. Make sure I'm easy to follow."

She purses her lips, her eyebrows pinching together before her features smooth out and she nods. "That sounds like the smart thing to do."

I stifle a snort.

I'm pretty sure the smart thing to do would be to stay far, far away from Lauren and focus on getting my life back together.

Good thing no one's ever accused me of being smart.

CHAPTER NINE

Lauren

The waitress clears our plates. "Can I interest either of you in dessert?"

"Depends," Jake replies. "Do you by chance have brownie sundaes?"

While I try my best not to, my gaze flicks to Jake. Heat curls low in my belly as a wicked grin curves his lips.

"We sure do." The waitress winks at Jake. "It's one of my favorites."

Jake meets my gaze. "Hers, too." His eyes narrow slightly. "One or two?"

"Huh?"

The corner of Jake's mouth hitches higher. "One or two? Are we sharing? Or do I need my own to avoid risking life and limb?"

"Ha-ha." I roll my eyes and bite back a smile.

"They're pretty big. Most people can't finish one on their own," the waitress says.

"Okay," Jake says. "One big brownie sundae, please." He raises an eyebrow at me. "As long as you promise not to stab me with a fork."

"I try not to make promises I can't keep."

The rumble of Jake's chuckle makes the heat swirl faster, and I cross my arms to keep the girls from showing him just what, exactly, he's doing to me. And while parts of me are definitely enjoying what he's doing, my brain is screaming to abort. Or to at least steer our conversation far away from the dangerous combination of chocolate and whipped cream and teasing. I'm just beginning to feel comfortable with him. I didn't even fumble over the whole practice teaching session thing. No telling how deep a pit I'll dig if we keep talking about dessert, though.

"So," I ask, after the waitress leaves, "how'd you get into the whole Motocross thing, anyway?" Good. That should be a safe topic.

"Kind of by accident, really." He shifts in his chair, a hint of a wry grin on his lips. "I was sort of a troublemaker growing up."

I flash him a look of mock surprise. "Really? Someone who races motorcycles for a living was a troublemaker? I never would've guessed."

His grin widens. "I started out doing stunts on my sister's banana seat bike, partly because I knew it pissed her off, and partly because I was actually good at it. Saved up for a couple of summers and got myself a ten-speed, and me and a couple of guys in the neighborhood built some jumps and made ourselves a little bike park. Drove our parents nuts, but it kept us out of worse trouble." He shrugs.

"When *that* thrill wore off, one of my buddies got a motorbike. I tried it, and I was hooked."

"And the whole professional athlete thing?"

"What about it?"

"Was that always your dream? Or did that happen by accident, too?"

"Both?" Jake wrinkles his nose. "I wasn't really good at school. Took my teachers a while to figure out that I have dyslexia, and even after they did, it was still much easier to be out racing than doing homework."

It's on the tip of my tongue to ask him what he'll do if he can't go back to racing, but the waitress returns and sets a gigantic brownie sundae between us. "Enjoy!" she says, laying two spoons on the table.

"Phew." Jake holds up one of the utensils. "At least if you decide to cause me bodily harm, it'll take you much more effort with this." He slides the other spoon toward me, then digs in. "So, was running the shop always *your* dream?"

My gaze snags on the way his lips wrap around the spoon, and I can almost feel any remaining brain cells shriveling up and dying.

Jake's eyebrow ticks upwards, amusement dancing in his eyes once again. "You okay over there?"

I shovel in a mouthful of the gooey concoction, partly to give myself time to recover, and partly because it really does look amazing. "What? Yeah. Great." Come on, Lauren. Don't go falling apart now. You're almost at the finish line. He asked you a question. Something about the shop. And your dreams. And he didn't mean dreaming about him in the shop, drizzled with the chocolate and whipped cream from the sundae.

Taking a sip of water, I shake my head. "No. Running the shop was always Kylie's thing. The plan was for Dad to run it until he was ready to retire, then for her to take over." The sugar rush takes a sudden nosedive as the memories resurface. "But then he died unexpectedly, and he left the shop to both of us."

"Were you working there before he died?"

"No. I worked in the finance office at the college. Still do, just part-time now." Although sometimes I seriously wonder if I won't need to go back and grovel for more hours sooner rather than later.

I squash the little flicker of resentment that makes an appearance every once in a blue moon. I'd been so close to that promotion.

"The things you do for family, right?"

I nod, and a few beats pass before I manage to find my voice. "Speaking of family. How about yours? Are your parents still around? Any other siblings?" Anything to get me out of the "what if" hole of my own life.

"No. Just me and Tracy. Our dad was never around much. He finally took off for good about twenty years ago—haven't heard from him since. Mom always worked several jobs, so Tracy kind of took on the mother role." His lips quirk. "Gave her a good reason to be bossy, I guess. Mom moved to New Mexico several years ago. Works at some resort-type thing outside Santa Fe."

"Ooh—I've always wanted to go to Santa Fe. Which resort? Maybe I should check it out. You know, if I ever get time off for a vacation."

"Bare Earth." Jake squirms, his lips twisted in a mixture of a wry smile and a grimace. "It's, uh, actually a nudist colony."

"Oh." Heat flares up my neck, partly at the thought of being naked in front of strangers, and partly at the thought of being naked in front of Jake. And vice versa. "Then never mind."

Jake shovels a bite of brownie into his mouth. "How about your mom? Is she around?"

"No. She died when I was in fifth grade. Went to sleep one night and didn't wake up. We think it was an aneurysm, but no one really knows for sure." Even though she's been gone for the better part of my life, the familiar ache blossoms in my chest.

"Oh, shit. I'm so sorry." Jake reaches across the table and lays a hand on my arm.

"Thanks."

We eat in silence for a few moments before Jake speaks again. "So, what do you do when you're *not* working at the shop?"

I relax into my seat again with the mention of a safer topic. "I love reading. And Sudoku."

"Sudo-what?"

"Sudoku. You know… Those number puzzles."

Jake's expression looks like he's just gotten a whiff of garbage.

"What? They're fun."

"Yeah. Right. Puzzles with math. I don't think so." He narrows his eyes at me. "If you tell me you were a Mathlete, I don't think we can be friends."

I press my lips together, and he heaves a theatrical sigh.

"Does it help if I got a varsity letter out of it?" I ask.

"Not one bit."

"You sound just like Kylie. She always made fun of me for it, too."

"For the record—" Jake holds up his empty spoon for emphasis. "—I did *not* make fun of you."

"Yeah. But I'll bet you were thinking it."

"I can neither confirm nor deny that accusation, under penalty of forking."

I roll my eyes. "It was *one* time, Kylie was annoying me, and we *don't even have forks*."

"True. But I know women. And women hold grudges. And there *will* come a day when you have access to a fork."

I raise my spoon to mirror him. "Or I *could* just spoon you now and be done with it."

Jake's eyebrow ticks upward, an interested gleam in his eye.

"With the spoon. Not, like, you know…" Shoot. And I was doing so well, too.

"Well, I can't talk about the silverware type of spooning, but for the record, I'm a fan of the other type."

I swallow, working hard to overcome the lust suddenly clogging my throat. "Good to know." Great. Yet another mental image to get out of my head.

Jake's phone buzzes, and he gives it a dirty look. "Looks like it's safe for me to head back to Tracy's again."

"Oh, good." Despite the fact that it means his nephew must be feeling better, disappointment flares at the thought that our evening is over.

Jake gives me a questioning look, and our waitress reappears. "Can I get you anything else?" She glances back and forth between us.

"No. Just the check, thanks," I reply.

"Hey, uh…" Jake rubs the back of his neck. "Thanks for keeping me company. And for the ride. I really appreciate it."

"It's the least I could do. Thanks again for all your help today. And for your ideas. I'm really looking forward to the teaching session. I think it'll be good for business."

Not to mention the fact that I have the sneaking suspicion it might just do wonders for my pleasure. And in this instance, mixing business with pleasure has the potential to be a brilliant idea.

I toss my purse on the coffee table before sprawling on my couch.

Despite the fact that I put my foot in my mouth on numerous occasions tonight, it actually wasn't the worst sort-of-but-not-really date I've ever had. Especially toward the end, when I started to calm down and began to see Jake as a guy. A totally hot guy, sure, but not the scary, intimidating guy I'd built him up to be. Just a regular guy with dyslexia and a hair-trigger vomit reflex who also happens to be a good-looking athlete.

And in *that* light, he seems much more approachable.

Not to mention the fact that unless I totally misread things, I think he was actually flirting with me. And I was flirting back. Badly, but still…

Wait. But what if he actually *wasn't* flirting? What if that was just Jake being Jake, and I'm overthinking things and end up making a total fool of myself?

Again.

Argh! Why can't I have a built-in gauge like Megan? She always knows which guys are into her. Although, to be fair, most guys seem to be interested in her. Of course, that could be because she doesn't go around admitting that her hobbies include reading and Sudoku. Or that she was a Mathlete.

Ugh.

Buzzing from the coffee table diverts my attention from the confusion swirling through my head.

Anyone else sending me a text with "911" as the message would be worrisome, but the fact that it comes from Megan is sadly routine. We've been using this as the code for "I need an extraction from a bad date" for so long now that heaven help her if she ever does have a true emergency.

While part of me considers ignoring it, a larger part of me is grateful for the respite. If I'm lucky, it'll trigger a cease-fire in the argument waging between reason and hope. Or at least cause a temporary truce.

I call her back, and she immediately picks up. "Lauren. What's wrong? Why are you crying?"

A mental image of Megan giving her date a helpless look plays in my mind's eye.

"Hang on, I'll be right there," she adds, hanging up without a word from me. About a minute later, she calls again. "Hey. Thanks. Dude would *not* shut up about his Star Trek bobblehead collection. How I missed *those* warning signs, I'll never know…" She sighs. "What're you up to? Want to hang out? Or do you need some Lauren time?"

I consider her questions. While it *has* been a really long day, and I *have* been itching to start that new Charlotte Nichols book, Megan and I haven't had time to catch up since the night at the bar. Plus, this is the perfect opportunity to go right to the master. See what she has to say about the whole flirting thing. "I think I'm in for the night, but come on over. And bring wine."

Ten minutes later, I'm in my PJs, Megan's kicked off her heels, and we're both reclining on my sofa with a glass of Malbec.

"So, what's new? Anything exciting going on?"

I study the surface of my drink. Be cool. "Not much. Just work."

She crinkles her nose. "Things going okay with Jake? Or did he already quit?"

"No. He's still there. So far, so good."

"Well, I still think you guys are crazy for hiring him, but I know you were kind of desperate, so…" She lifts her shoulders, her expression saying "what can you do?"

"He's actually a really good employee. And a great mechanic. And a really nice guy."

"Wait." Megan's eyes narrow. "Please tell me you're not interested in Jake."

"What? Of course not. Why would you even think that?" Good thing my couch is flame-retardant, because my pajama pants are liable to burst into flames at any minute now.

Megan continues to study me, her lips pursed.

Crap. Maybe a little misdirection…

"But what if I *was* interested in someone?"

"Someone *not* Jake, right?"

"Definitely not Jake."

"Good. Because guys like him are total players."

My voice of reason pumps its fist in victory as hope tells it to shut up.

"Where'd did you meet this guy?" she continues.

Uh… Come on, Lauren. Think. Something close enough to the truth to make it believable. Truth-adjacent. "At the shop. A customer. Comes in sometimes for repairs and equipment." Yeah. Good. Totally plausible. "But I can't tell if he's interested, or if he's just a flirt and acts like that with all women."

Megan givens me another long look, then nods, a mixture of relief and excitement on her face. "Well, Grasshopper, you've come to the right place."

CHAPTER TEN

Jake

Lauren licks a fudge smear off her lower lip, her eyes riveted to mine before she leans forward and trails her tongue back down my abdomen.

She traces a path due south, my groin tightening in anticipation. I shudder.

"Uncle Jake?"

Biting back a groan, I will her to keep working her magic. Those lips, that tongue—

"Uncle Jake? Why are you making those noises? Are you hurt again?"

Reality rudely replaces my lust-filled dreams as I peel one eyelid open. My nephew's brown eyes peer at me over the edge of my bed. "What? No. I'm fine." Disappointed and uncomfortable, but otherwise okay.

"Good. Hey, Uncle Jake."

"Hey, Reece's Pieces."

"Guess what? I frowed up yesterday. A lot."

"Yeah. I know. Your mom told me. You feeling better today?" I lift my head to get a better look.

His cowlick bobs as he nods. "Yep. I'm hungry, too. Mom's making pancakes. She told me to come get you."

"Ah." That explains the wake-up call.

His little eyebrows furrow as I shift in bed. "What's that?" He points to the continued evidence of my sex dreams tenting the sheet.

"Uh…"

"Is that your penis?" Curious eyes bore into mine.

"Uh-huh."

"Why is it standing up? How can I get mine to stand up? Can I teach it to do tricks?" Reece's eyes disappear, the crown of his head appearing in their place, and I have no doubt my nephew is now exploring the snake in his underpants.

Tracy keeps saying it's just a phase, that he'll outgrow the "self-exploration phase," as she calls it. Poor, deluded psychologist. As a man, I know better. He'll be playing with that thing until he dies.

"Go tell your mom I'll be out soon. And, uh, don't mention the tricks, okay?" Don't need another reason for Tracy to start harping on me.

"Okay!" Reece's tiny footsteps fade as he runs toward the kitchen. "Hey, Mom! Guess what? Uncle Jake's penis stands up!"

So much for keeping secrets.

I make my way out of bed, my thoughts boomeranging back to Lauren as I go through the tedious task of getting dressed.

How much I enjoyed hanging out with her, both during the event and after.

How much I liked seeing the real her begin to peek through.

How for the first time in a long time I've actually wanted to get to know a woman on a deeper level. Although, her deeper levels are kind of intimidating. I mean, even her *hobbies* are smart. What the hell would she want with a dyslexic guy who may or may not be a washed-up athlete in the near future?

But that doesn't mean she and I can't have a little fun in the meantime. Assuming she *does* want to have fun. Although, maybe she doesn't. I mean, I thought we were flirting and connecting, but then when Tracy texted it seemed like Lauren was relieved that the night was over.

Damn. Maybe she's not as into me as I thought.

The idea halts me on the way to the bathroom.

Shit. What if she was just being nice?

I give my head a quick shake.

Dude. Stop it. Stop overthinking things.

I stifle a snort.

Pretty sure I've never been accused of overthinking anything before in my life. Of course, maybe a little overthinking would've kept my leg in one piece...

Blowing out a breath, I try to recenter my thoughts. Something I do before races to get my head in the proper place. Because I don't know where it is now, but it's nowhere helpful, that's for damn sure.

What I need is to focus on something other than my confusing thoughts. Except the place that gives me the best chance of keeping my mind occupied is also the place I have the best chance of being distracted.

Damn. I really should've thought this whole thing through more.

Kylie wheels a bike into the shop and props it against the counter, then leans next to it. "I hear things went pretty well yesterday."

"Yeah. I obviously have nothing to compare it to, but I think so." Especially the after part. I work to keep my expression neutral. "I had a good time."

A crease forms between Kylie's eyebrows. "Yeah. So did Lauren. Which is weird..." She shrugs, her expression smoothing out. "So, whatever you did, good job."

Smug satisfaction washes over me. Maybe I'm not overthinking things after all. "Is she coming in today?"

Kylie shrugs again. "Not sure. She usually works from home on Sundays, but she *has* been here a little more than usual, so who knows?"

Interesting. I tuck that nugget away, giving a noncommittal head bob as I make another slight adjustment to the brake line of the bike I'm working on.

Kylie scuffs the toe of her sneaker against the floor. "So, uh, I just wanted to say thank you."

"You're welcome." Testing the brake line again, I tighten the barrel adjusters a few additional degrees. "What exactly for?"

"For stepping up. I kind of threw you and Lauren under the bus with the event yesterday. But from what I'm hearing, you guys did really well, and I'm impressed with your ideas about adding classes. Not only that, but the customers love your work, and you've managed to get the shop somewhat organized, too."

"Yeah, well, what can I say? Idle hands, yada, yada." I grin. "But thanks. It feels good to be a productive member of society again." Or maybe for the first time, seeing as how Motocross Racer isn't always seen as the most worthwhile career.

She tilts her head to the side and studies me. "I am definitely willing to extend our agreement past the trial period. How about you?"

"Absolutely." Part of the uncertainty that's been sitting in my gut for the last few weeks dissolves. It may not be a permanent solution, but at least for the foreseeable future I should have a steady stream of income. Not to mention something to look forward to.

"Good. Then it's a deal." She holds out her hand, and we shake. "Just promise me you won't up and leave without fair warning."

"Got it."

Kylie nods. "I'll leave you to it, then." She pushes off from the counter and heads toward the door, stopping at the edge of the room. With a sigh, she turns around. "And don't take this the wrong way. I'm definitely not interested, and you're not exactly Lauren's type, but after what happened with me and AJ... Workplace romances? Not a good idea."

Shit. Does she know I'm interested in her sister? Doesn't look like it. She's not giving me the death glare she had going on when we first met. Looks more like she's relieved to have said it. Probably just trying to cover her bases. Or what's that thing Tracy says about people sometimes? Oh, right. Maybe she's projecting. Or is it transferring?

Damn. I have definitely been hanging around my sister too long.

Whatever the hell it is Kylie's doing, no doubt my best bet is to just go ahead and agree with her. "I'll try to keep from hitting on your Uncle Pete."

She snorts.

And then, because her words niggle at my pea-brain, I feel obligated to continue the conversation. "But out of curiosity? What exactly *is* Lauren's type?"

Kylie's eyes narrow.

Good job, Jake. Way to quit while you're ahead. *Not.* That sounded way too much like personal interest. I need a diversion. "She and Spencer were quite chatty yesterday. Is *he* her type?"

As expected, the mention of Spencer tightens Kylie's jaw to the point that I wouldn't be surprised if she cracked a tooth. "No," she grinds out. "Lauren tends to go for the nerdy, smarty-pants type. Not the ultra-competitive assholes who wouldn't know good sense if it hit them over the head." She shakes her head as if trying to clear it. "But, uh, would you let me know if you see anything funny going on between them?"

"Absolutely." I am definitely more than happy to pay closer attention to Lauren.

What I'm not quite so happy about is the fact that Kylie basically just described Lauren's type as the exact opposite of me. While I can't say that I'm surprised, it does lend extra support to that whole "Lauren was just being nice to me" argument. An argument I'm really starting to dislike, by the way.

But even though I might not be the smartest guy in the classroom, there's no doubt I'm determined. And right now, despite my conversation with Kylie, I'm determined to keep the pedal to the metal around Lauren.

After all, as hockey legend Wayne Gretzky said, "You miss one hundred percent of the shots you don't take." And I, for one, have never believed in playing it safe.

CHAPTER ELEVEN

Lauren

"Hey," Kylie says, restocking the bicycle glove displays. "Don't forget I've got indoor soccer tonight."

"Don't worry. I won't." Partly because she's been playing in that same league for years, and partly because it means Jake and I will be alone in the shop.

My pulse skitters at the thought.

Following the Pedals & Medals event, we've had several days of nonstop traffic. Which is great for business and the bottom line, but lousy when all you want to do is have that damn hands-on session with the hot mechanic in the back room.

But it looks like I might finally get my chance. Not only is tonight usually our quiet night, but it's starting to drizzle. Not too many bike emergencies when it's raining out.

"How about you?" Kylie asks. "Any big plans for tonight?"

My eyes snap from the computer screen to my sister, and I can feel the heat gathering at my neck. "What? No. Why?" I squeak.

Yeah. Way to keep cool.

Kylie's face pinches into one of her "what the hell" expressions. "Geez. What's with you?"

"Nothing. I'm fine."

"Uh-huh." Her eyes narrow slightly.

Damn. My sister can be like a dog with a bone sometimes. Don't need her poking around right now. I'm jumpy enough already. No telling what I'd let slip in my current state of mind.

While sometimes it's a pain in the butt knowing each other so well, it comes in handy in times like this. Because I know just how to misdirect her. "Hey, uh, which team are you guys playing tonight?"

She all but snarls and grinds out "Spencer's." Just like I knew she would. She's been muttering about it all week.

Making a show of looking at my watch, I shake my head. "You should probably get going, then. Don't want to be late. No telling what Spence would say if you missed your game." I pull my face into a wince. "He might think you're scared to play him."

Her nostrils flare, and she slams the last of the gloves onto the rack. "Oh, *hell* no. I'm out. See you tomorrow. Gotta go kick some ass."

I bite my lip to keep my smile in check until after she's stormed out the front door. Honestly—sometimes, she's just too easy.

My glee at outwitting my sister takes a backseat to the queasy giddiness at the reminder that I'm now here in the shop with Jake. Alone.

My heartrate climbs another octave.

Okay, Lauren. You can do this. Be cool. Just go back and ask him if he's available for that teaching session tonight. No big deal.

Yeah. Right. And I'm a mechanical genius.

Shaky legs carry me to the back of the shop, my knees becoming even more Jell-O-like when Jake looks up and grins. "Hey. What's up?"

"Hey. So, uh…" I ball my hands into fists and gulp down the rising nerves. "I was wondering if maybe you wanted to test out those hands-on teaching sessions tonight. With me. Unless you have other stuff to do?" Shit. What if he has other stuff to do?

Jake nods, his grin widening. "Yeah. Absolutely."

"Absolutely you want to do the session? Or absolutely you have other stuff to do?"

"The first thing."

"Oh. Good." I blow out a breath. One step down. The problem is, now we're onto step two. And if I was that nervous with step one, step two's liable to make me pass out. And poor Jake wouldn't even be much help. Unless I need CPR.

Ooh. CPR. The kiss of life. Well, in that case, maybe unconsciousness wouldn't be so bad. Does mouth-to-mouth count as a first kiss?

"Lauren?"

I blink, the mental image of Jake's lips on mine fading away as reality takes hold. "What?"

"I asked if you're okay over there."

"Oh. Yeah. Sure. Great." If you don't count the fact that I'm an awkward nutjob who's hot for an employee.

"Alright." He juts his chin toward the front of the store. "Kylie still here?"

"Nope. It's just you and me."

Jake nods, silence filling the space between us.

"Unless you don't want it to be. Should we wait for Kylie?" The words burst out of my mouth before I can stop them.

Confusion mars Jake's features. "No. Not on my account. Unless *you* want to wait for Kylie?"

"No. I'm good with just the two of us. As long as you are, of course."

Jake's features soften. "Me too."

"Plus, she already knows this stuff," I add, waving my hand toward the bike in front of him.

"Right."

"So it makes sense for it to be just us."

"Of *course,* it does."

I study Jake, trying to figure out if he's mocking me, agreeing with me, or placating me. Probably some combination. But right now, I'm not all that sure I care. Because Jake's free, we're alone, and it's time to get this show on the road.

Oh, boy.

Jake grins again and tilts his head, nodding me closer to where he's seated. "I'm ready if you are."

I gulp, my heart tap dancing in my chest. Okay, Lauren. Time to learn some stuff about bikes and figure out a little more about what makes Jake tick. Time to see if he's simply being nice and helpful, if he's just being a big flirt, or if he's really into you.

Please let it be the last one.

Let's see… What the hell did hell did Megan say? Something about touching. And listening? Or was that when she was trying to teach *me* how to flirt? Crap!

Jake clears his throat. "I think it'll be more effective if you come over here."

A nervous laugh tumbles past my lips, and I will my body across the floor, planting myself next to him. On the plus side, I'm no longer distracted by his sparkling eyes or his kissable lips. On the down side, he smells really good. Like a mixture of citrus and the forest after a rainstorm. It's both relaxing and stimulating all at the same time.

Argh! This is gonna be torture!

Jake points to the bike on the stand in front of us. "This guy, here, is in serious need of a new chain."

"Oh, no." Maybe this wasn't such a brilliant idea after all.

"Yeah. He really is."

"No. I mean, chains and I don't get along." Usually it's *my* fingers that end up getting pinched or cut, but there were more than a few times when Dad's or Kylie's digits took the brunt of my ineptitude. Shoot. I should've thought of that before going all gung-ho. Poor Jake can't really afford to sacrifice any more body parts.

"So what we're gonna do," he continues before I can lodge any further protest, "is pop this one off and give him a new one. Nothing to it."

"Yeah. Speak for yourself." I stare at my old nemesis, my brain working overtime to find additional reasons why this is a bad idea. "Wait. So, if we show the customers how to do this type of stuff, why would they keep coming back to have us do it?" Damn. I *really* should've thought this through a little more. Here I'd been so eager to spend more time with Jake that I didn't stop to think about what his idea might actually do to our business.

"Simple." Jake winks. "Convenience. People might want to *see* what I'm doing, but rarely are they actually gonna decide to do it for themselves. Think about our culture—it's all convenience these days."

He does have a point there. Plus, there is the whole possibility that people might come *specifically* to watch Jake work. I mean, I definitely would.

"So, anyway," Jake continues, "first order of business—pop the old chain off." He plucks a tool from the bench next to him and hands it to me. "Okay. Show me what you've got."

What I've got is a sinking feeling that tonight is going to be a lot more work than I'd bargained for.

"Dammit!" Every time. Why can I never remember how to thread the new chain through the rear derailleur? It's like my kryptonite.

"Okay. Easy there, killer. Slow down." Jake places a hand on mine, preventing me from continuing to trying to yank the chain in a way it clearly doesn't want to go. "This part can be tricky. Just take your time."

I blow out a breath, trying equally to maintain my cool over the stubborn bike part and to keep my heart from thudding through my rib cage. Because little tingles of pleasant electricity radiate from our points of contact.

"Want me to help?"

I nod at Jake's question, not trusting myself to open my mouth right now.

"Okay." He shifts beside me, his good leg resting against mine.

Great. Even more points of contact to turn my brain cells to mush.

"What you want to do..." He leans over and places his free hand on my other one, then shakes his head. "That's not gonna work."

"Why not?" On the contrary—I'm all for three points of contact.

"I'm liable to pull a back muscle that way. Hold on. I've got a better idea." He stands up and maneuvers behind me on his crutches. "Okay. Let's try this again. Gimme your hands."

Ooh, this is *definitely* a better idea. The solid muscles of Jake's chest press against my back as his strong hands take mine. His breath whispers soft caresses across the ultra-sensitive skin of my neck.

Full body contact for the win.

He guides my hands through the remainder of the task, and despite the fact that he's keeping a running commentary on what he's doing, there is no way I'd be able to do it on my own. My brain cells are currently on vacation, doing lazy laps in the hormone pool.

And they're loving it.

"See?" Jake says. "That wasn't so bad, was it?"

"Definitely not." My muscles relax into him, craving even more contact. "I could stay like this all day." Wait. Did I say that last part out loud?

"Oh, yeah? Well, I can't." Jake shifts behind me, and before I know what's happened, he's tugged me around. He repositions his crutches, his gaze darting back and forth between my eyes and my lips. His Adam's apple bobs as he swallows, and he licks his lips and oh, holy hell, is Jake about to kiss me?

The pressure of his lips on mine drives away any further questions. Unless you count the one about wondering if I've died and gone to heaven. Because I'm pretty sure this is what heaven's like—Jake's mouth slanted across mine, his lips equal parts gentle and demanding. His tongue darting out as if it's on an exploratory mission in search of new and exciting treasures. His calloused hand gently cupping the back of my neck. Pleasure tingles erupting like little celebratory hormone fireworks.

Okay. I was wrong before. *This* is how I could spend all day.

Kissing Jake.

Our new employee.

In the back of our shop.

Our *family* shop.

Just like Kylie and AJ.

Oh, God. What have I done?

CHAPTER TWELVE

Jake

Oh, yeah. This is much better.

Don't get me wrong. Having Lauren leaning into me, guiding her hands through the remainder of the new chain tutorial was great, but it was driving me crazy. That same damned whiff of vanilla shampoo or body lotion that makes me want to do some very naughty things with my tongue. The curves that fit so nicely against me. The way she trusted me and seemed to relax and enjoy herself.

But the way her lips part for mine, inviting me in. The way her tongue caresses mine, almost as if in tentative greeting. The little breathy moans of pleasure I'm not sure she knows she's making.

This is the good stuff.

Except…wait. Why is she tensing up all of a sudden? And why did she stop kissing me?

Lauren's eyes pop open, and she pulls her hands off me like I'm a hot engine. "We shouldn't've done that."

I fight to keep my balance, my center of gravity thrown off by her sudden distance. Or maybe from the kiss. Possibly both. "Why not?"

The pink on her cheeks deepens, and her eyes dart around the room. "Uh…"

Shit. She's doing that thing she does when she's uncomfortable. Did I move too fast? Or maybe I really *have* been reading this whole situation wrong. Kylie's words about Lauren and her type zoom through my brain like a biker headed for the finish line.

Dammit, Jake. You're not her type. *And* she's your boss. Way to leap before you look. *Again.* You are *so* getting fired.

My typical bravado deflates like a leaky tire. "Lauren—"

Her eyes snap to mine, and she holds up a hand. "Wait." Her bottom lip disappears between her teeth for a few beats before she seems to steel herself, her spine straightening. "Why did you kiss me?"

"Is this a trick question?"

Her hair swings as she shakes her head back and forth.

"Uh…" Crap. This still feels like a trick question. But Lauren doesn't seem like someone who plays games. And I don't either. "Because I like you."

"You do?"

"Yeah."

She rolls her lip between her teeth again, this time, a smile tilting the corners of her mouth.

"But don't worry. I won't kiss you again."

Her eyebrows lower, the hint of a smile disappearing. "Why not?"

"Because you just said that we shouldn't."

Her mouth rounds into an O before something that looks like regret washes over her face. "I'm your boss."

"Uh-huh." For now, anyway. Until she fires my ass.

"And Kylie and I made a pact that we wouldn't date employees." Her face reddens even further. "Not that you and I would ever date. Just... You know..."

"Yeah." I know. My typical M.O. is more like a sprint. Never been a marathon-type guy. Plus, she should be with someone smart. Not someone who barely managed to graduate high school.

"And even without the whole Kylie-AJ thing, workplace romances are a bad idea." She winces.

Her words roll around in my head like they're circling a training oval. Huh. Of all her protests, not a one involved her not being attracted to me. Interesting. "Well, for the record, I happen to agree with you."

Disappointment flickers across her face. "You do?"

I nod, my bravado slowly regathering steam. "Yep. Workplace romances *are* a bad idea. In fact, I've avoided them up to now. Of course, that *could* be because the guys on tour don't smell nearly as good as you and have a little too much body hair for my taste."

Lauren dips her head, the flush returning to her cheeks as she fights a smile.

"And I totally get the whole wanting to play by the rules stuff. I do." Kind of. From her standpoint, anyway. "So just say the word, and this never happened." As much as I would love to pick up right where we left off, I'll leave her alone if she wants me to.

God, I hope she doesn't want me to leave her alone.

My words hang between us as Lauren's hands ball into fists, her shoulders rising and falling as she takes several deep breaths. Closing her eyes, she swallows, then latches her gaze onto mine with one final exhale. "No."

I do my best Professor-X impersonation, trying to read her thoughts, but come up empty. "No, what?"

"No, I don't want that to have not happened." She gives her head a quick shake. "I mean, I'm *glad* it happened. I'm tired of being the good girl. Always playing by the rules." A mixture of hope and uncertainty gathers on her features. "I'd like for it to happen again."

My misgivings fall by the wayside, and I can feel the grin spreading across my face. "Happy to oblige."

I lean in again, but she places a hand on my chest. "Seriously, though. I *am* gonna need to draw something up HR-wise."

"Not a problem. Just tell me where to sign."

"And you *cannot* tell Kylie."

"Don't worry. I won't." Don't need to get on *her* bad side. Not with how long she holds a grudge.

Desire flickers in her eyes, and she swallows. "Okay, then. As long as we're both agreed…" Her eyes dip to my mouth, and before I can blink, she's pressed against me, her lips and tongue picking up where they left off. This time, with a little less hesitation and a little more assertiveness.

Sweet yet decisive.

I like it.

What I don't like is the fact that as Lauren leans more of her weight into me, my good leg starts to protest, and my precarious balance gets even more squirrely. If I don't do something now, we might both end up on the ground. And not for the reason I'd like us to wind up horizontal. "Uh… Lauren?"

"Hmm?" she all but purrs.

My leg wobbles, and the hand still on my crutch tightens around the handle while the hand threaded through her hair drops, redistributing some of my weight onto her shoulder.

She blinks, our lips now unlocked, confusion slowly replaced by an expression somewhere between apology and chagrin as my crutch clatters on the ground.

I take a few small hops in an attempt to regain my balance. "I really don't want to break up this party, but…"

She winces. "No, *I'm* sorry. I might've been a little overenthusiastic."

"Believe me. That was just the right amount of enthusiasm."

She helps me crutch-hop to the stool, and I sit down while she gets the fallen crutch. "And for the record, I am totally pissed at my body right now." I mean, I practically cockblocked myself. How is that even possible?

"Well, to be fair, it *has* been through a lot lately."

"True." I roll my shoulders and try to stretch out my back. While several parts of me enjoyed what just happened with Lauren, the muscles in those areas weren't among them.

Lauren gives me a shy smile, the stain on her cheeks intensifying. "If it helps, I'm really good at backrubs."

"Oh, yeah?"

"Uh-huh." She wiggles her fingers. "Kylie and Megan say these things are practically magic."

Oh, holy crap. This woman's gonna be the death of me.

But at least I'll die a happy man.

CHAPTER THIRTEEN

Lauren

Holy crap!

First you're kissing Hot Jake. Now you're giving him a back massage. What the hell has gotten into you?

I bite back a laugh, but apparently not well enough, because Jake turns his head. "Everything okay back there?"

"Yep." If you don't count the fact that I may or may not have suffered a complete mental breakdown. "How about with you?"

"Fantastic." Jake hisses out a breath as I dig into yet another knot.

"Yeah," I say, my fingers pausing. "Sounds like it."

"Seriously. It's great. Don't stop." He dips his head, and the muscles under my hands expand as he takes another breath. Silence hangs in the room, punctuated occasionally by Jake's contented sighs, until he speaks again. "You know, if I wind up going back on tour, I may have to take you with me."

"If?"

His shoulders bunch, relaxing as he lets out a sigh equal parts weariness and disgust. "Yeah. I don't know if I'm gonna be able to ride again after this." He pats his cast.

"Why not? I mean, it's early yet, right?"

"Yeah. But I've known other guys who've messed up their legs, some of them not even this bad, who couldn't make it back. Plus, I'm old."

"No, you're not. We're practically the same age."

"Yeah. But in Motocross years, I'm kind of over the hill."

"Well, you look really good for your age."

He huffs a soft laugh but otherwise remains silent.

While part of me wants to offer additional encouragement, I also don't want to offer false hope. Especially since I know nothing about his world. And I can't even imagine what it would be like to have to give up your livelihood. Well, I mean, I can. I kind of did. But I had a choice. Sort of.

"Anyway," Jake says. "Enough about me and my future. Or lack thereof. I want to hear more about you being done with the whole 'playing by the rules' thing."

My hands still on his neck. Crap. Did I let that part slip, too? Should've known he was paying closer attention to what I said than I was.

Jake swivels, angling so he can see me. "You know, if you need some help in that department, I know someone who might be interested."

Dammit! Why does he have to be so attractive? And funny? And nice? Why can't I just get it through my head that this is a seriously bad idea and walk away?

Probably because Jake's attractive, funny, and nice.

It also doesn't help that things have begun to niggle at my brain like little insects trying to find a home. Like the fact that it's not fair that I'm always the one to do the right thing. Following the rules and staying out of trouble growing up. Coming back to work at the shop after Dad died. Helping at the Pedals & Medals event so Kylie wouldn't have to.

Okay. Not like that last one was exactly a hardship, but still. It's the principle of the matter.

Not that there's anything wrong with being a good person. It's who I am. But I deserve to have a little fun now and then, too, dammit. Besides, Kylie's not the boss of me. Why should I suffer because of something she did? That's not fair.

Neither is the fact that Jake continues to send his smoldering gaze my way.

I mean, how's a girl supposed to fight *that*?

And what kind of person would even *want* to?

A crazy one, that's who.

My heart beats in my throat as I weigh my resolve to stay in my good girl lane with the tug to expand my horizons with Jake. I bark out a laugh at the euphemism. I'll bet a lot of women would like Jake to expand their horizons.

Jake shifts, uncertainty clouding his features. "Do I want to know what's going on in that gigantic brain of yours right now?"

"I don't have a gigantic brain."

"Please. I can see you overthinking things from over here."

I scoff. "I do *not* overthink things."

Jake levels me with a bland look. "Right. Just like I don't underthink things." His forehead wrinkles. "Is that a word? Anyway. You know what I mean."

A resigned sigh escapes. How does he already know me so well? "Fine. My *gigantic brain* is busy arguing with itself about what it wants to do."

"About?"

I gulp. "You."

His eyebrow ticks upward. "Because…?"

My pulse pounds in my ears, and I lean against the counter just in case my nervous system decides to go on strike. Okay. Time to put up or shut up. "Because I really like you and I think you like me too but I shouldn't like you because of the business and Kylie and Megan although I deserve to have a little fun and they can just go to hell." I wince. "In a nutshell."

A laugh rumbles in Jake's chest. "Feel better now?"

I scrunch my nose. "Maybe."

He grins. "Good. And for the record, I *do* like you, and my offer to help you have a little fun still stands."

"Even if my gigantic brain is full of overthinking crazy?"

"*Especially* if your gigantic brain is full of overthinking crazy. Seriously. I think I got here just in time. No telling what'll happen if you don't let some steam off once in a while."

Hmm. When he says it like that, it almost makes sense. I won't be good to anyone if I explode. Maybe it *is* in everyone's best interests if Jake helps me unwind. Speaking of which, since everything seems to be out in the open now, maybe we could try unwinding a little more…

The sound of the front door opening and closing drags me back to reality.

I sigh. "Of course. Just when things were getting good."

Jake reaches out and wraps his hand around my wrist, one side of his mouth cocked upward. Little shivers dance along the points of contact. "Just remember. I'm here to help."

As if I could forget.

CHAPTER FOURTEEN

Jake

Life is good.

Well, not totally sucking anyway, which is an improvement from a month ago.

I'm enjoying my job, Lauren and I finally seem to be on the same page interest-wise, and I'm about to get my big-ass cast replaced by a smaller one. Hopefully.

Dr. Anderson sits down on the stool across from me and nods. "Good news, Jake—we're going to change you to a below-the-knee cast today."

Relief whooshes out of me like a gashed tire. "Thank God. That means I'm on schedule, right? That I should get back to riding again by next year?" Even the thought of having to wait *that* long threatens to send me over the Cliffs of Insanity, but I guess it's better than the alternative.

He shakes his head, his typically stoic expression firmly in place. "Not sure yet. The break near your knee looks like it's healing well, but your ankle isn't quite as far along as I'd hoped. We'll re-evaluate with another set of x-rays in four weeks."

Tension creeps back into my shoulders as I stare at my leg. Relax. You're fine. Not the worst news he could've given me, but not the best, either.

"Hang in there. Some people just take longer than others to heal." He taps a few notes on his computer, then glances up. "Not that I didn't do a good job with your ankle repair, but Jake... Have you given any thought to retiring?"

Shit, shit, shit. My chest squeezes, and I gulp down the panic and dread rising in my throat. *Definitely* not how I was hoping this visit would go.

He raises a hand as if to stop my thoughts from speeding out of control. "Not that I see anything right now that would prevent you from returning, but I just want to make sure you know what you're in for with trying to make a comeback. It's going be a long, hard road. And even then—no guarantees."

His words buzz through my head like a swarm of angry bees while the medical assistant changes my cast. Retiring. No guarantees.

And even though my leg feels lighter when she's done, his words continue to weigh on me. Because he's right. What if I put in all the hard work to attempt a comeback and I'm still not good enough? I was barely good enough before. What if all I do is end up wasting time I could've used to get on with my life? I don't know which choice would make me the bigger idiot—going for the comeback or deciding to move on.

My thoughts continue to circle like a driver doing donuts as I wait outside the surgeon's office. Testing my knee again, I grimace. Fuck, that hurts. But at least I can bend it now. Kind of. And it doesn't feel like I'm lugging around a concrete block anymore. Well, not a big one, anyway.

Tracy pulls up to the curb, rolls down the passenger window, and whistles. "Looking good!"

I give her a half-hearted smile, folding myself into the seat beside her for the first time since my injury. "Thanks."

"Blue this time, huh?"

"Yep."

"Nice. Reece will love it. How's it feel?"

"Leg feels lighter. Knee hurts like a mother. Doc says it should get better. That it's just stiff." I test my joint again, grimacing as it moves like the rusty hinge that it is. "He gave me some exercises to try to get a little strength and range of motion back."

"That's good. How's the ankle?"

I shrug. "We'll see."

Tracy's brows draw together as she studies me. "You okay? I expected you to be a little more upbeat since you graduated to the new cast."

My head drops onto the headrest, and I push away another round of woe-is-me. "Yeah. I'm fine."

"Coulda fooled me."

"It's just…" I force a swallow past the uncertainty still lodged in my throat. "Doc said my ankle's not quite healing like he was hoping. And he, uh, asked if I'd been thinking of retiring." My words catch, and I force in a breath. "What if I really am done racing?" I know I've said it out loud before, but for the first time, it seems like it might actually be true.

Her eyebrows scrunch together, concern and surprise warring on her features. "Seriously?"

I shrug again, giving my lip a workout with my teeth.

"Wow. That would be…huge."

"Yeah."

"*Are* you done racing?"

"I don't know."

After a few moments of silence, she squeezes my shoulder. "Hey. It's okay. Just know that whatever you decide, you're still my brother. And I'm here for you. *We're* here for you."

"Thanks." I gulp down another surge of emotions. When I'm no longer in danger of letting any rogue feelings leak out, I tack on, "You mean, you're not gonna boss me around and throw in your two cents? Who are you, and what have you done with my sister?"

"Well, *of course*, I'm gonna boss you around. That's my job. But as for the second thing? Nope—not my two cents to give."

A half-hearted laugh huffs out of me. "What kind of psychologist are you, anyway?"

"The kind who believes in you."

Great. That makes one of us.

All I can say is thank God for this job.

I considered going home after my appointment, but I have no doubt that stewing in my own juices would've only made my confusion, not to mention my mood, that much worse. Throwing myself into the shop's work orders goes a long way toward helping me sweep aside the questions about my future.

Well, work and Lauren. Or, more specifically, that kiss.

Even though she's not at the shop, my brain keeps rewinding to the other night. How good it finally felt to have her lips on mine. To feel her soft curves pressed against me. To feel her begin to let loose.

Makes me itch to get her alone again. When we're not in danger of having someone walk in on us.

"Wow." Kylie ambles into the room, nodding appreciatively as she looks around. "Someone's gunning for Employee of the Month. I kind of hate to break whatever mojo you've got going on, but it's closing time."

Damn. So soon?

I test out the brake lines of my latest victim, making a few additional tweaks. "Alright. I just need a few more minutes, then this one's done, too."

And then I can go home. Where Tracy may or may not be lying in wait to psychoanalyze me and my future plans. Or maybe if I'm lucky, Reece will insist on another rousing game of Candy Land tonight.

Ugh. I really need to get out more.

"Okay. Good." Kylie tilts her head and narrows her eyes. "Hey. You wanna join me and Lauren? We're meeting for karaoke after I close up."

"Uh, I don't wanna break up Girls' Night."

She waves her hand as if swatting away my words. "Nah. You're not breaking anything up. It's actually kind of a celebration. And since you're a part of the team now, you should come."

The potential for a Lauren smile at the end of a crappy day? Additional distractions from my questionable future? The potential for another entertaining Kylie karaoke night?

Hell, yeah. Sign me up.

"So?" Kylie asks. "What do you say? You in?"

"Yep. I'm in."

Possibly way over my head.

CHAPTER FIFTEEN

Lauren

I look up from my phone, surprised to see Megan plopping down next to me. "Hey. What are you doing here? I thought you had a date."

"I do." She glances over to the bar and winks at the new bartender.

I roll my eyes. "So help me, if you get us barred from this place…"

Megan shakes her head. "Not with him. With Zane. I'm meeting him at Calhoun's. Popped in to say hi while I wait." She swipes my wine and takes a sip, her eyes lighting up. "So… How'd it go with *your* guy? Any headway? Did you figure out what his deal is?"

Ugh. Should've known she'd be hungry for details. Why didn't I work on my story?

Because I've been too busy daydreaming, that's why. Wondering if Jake's thinking about our kiss as much as I have. Fantasizing about how his mouth would feel on other parts of my body. Imagining his strong hands grasping my—

"Ooh!" Megan breathes. "Spill!"

"What?"

"You've got dreamy sex eyes. What happened? Spill it!"

I squirm in my seat, willing my body to calm down. "I do not have dreamy sex eyes. Nothing happened."

Megan's gaze sharpens.

Dammit. She's like a lie-seeking missile. "Okay. We kissed."

"And?"

"And that's all."

"Hmmm." A knowing smile teases her lips. "But it was good, right?"

Despite my best attempts at holding it in, my enthusiasm gushes out. "Oh, my God. It was amazing. The best kiss I've ever had."

The Cheshire Cat grin spreads. "Good for you. So? What's the next step?"

"What's the next step for what?" Kylie asks from behind us.

Crap.

I give Megan a pleading look, but she's never been big on keeping secrets.

"Lauren and her lover."

"Her *what*?" Kylie's head whips to me. "What the hell? When did this happen?"

The glee in Megan's eyes at divesting a juicy piece of gossip dies, her face hardening as she looks at something past Kylie. "What's *he* doing here?"

Looking around Kylie, I see Jake a few steps away.

Oh, holy hell. How much did he hear?

"He's part of our team, and I invited him." Kylie shrugs. Her eyes sharpen as she turns her attention back to me. "But back to the whole 'lover' thing…"

"I don't have a lover."

Do not look at Jake, do not look at Jake, do not look at Jake.

"Fine," Megan huffs. "Your kisser." She sighs and bats her lashes. "Best kiss ever."

Despite my attempt to keep my eyes on Kylie and Megan, they slide to Jake. While my face feels like it could spontaneously combust from excessive heat, his looks like he's actually enjoying himself. Amusement and interest dance in his eyes, and he fails to keep the self-satisfied smile off his face.

My heart trips over itself, but I'm not sure if it's because of how good he looks or because we're this close to someone stumbling upon what we did.

"Who is he?" asks Kylie.

What the hell did I tell Megan the other night? Oh, right. I told her it was a customer. Shit. Why didn't I say it was someone from the college?

"Uh… A customer?"

Confusion clouds Kylie's features. "Really? Which one?"

"Is it that annoying guy with the flip glasses and the goatee? It's totally him, isn't it?" Jake asks, taking a seat next to me.

I'm not sure if I want to kiss him for trying to deflect suspicion away from the two of us or smack him for adding fuel to the fire. Probably a little of both.

"None of you have met him. Now. Can we *please* discuss something other than my love life?" I scowl at Megan. "And shouldn't you be leaving?"

I can almost see the gears turning in Megan's head, trying to figure out if she'd rather stay to pry additional information out of me or leave for her date. "Fine." She gives Jake a frosty look, then turns her attention back to me as she stands up. "But we are *not* finished with this discussion."

"Yeah. Seriously," adds Kylie. "What the hell? What happened to our no relationship pact?"

I squirm in my seat. "It's not a relationship! We just kissed. Geez!" Despite the gravitational pull toward Jake, I keep my eyes trained on my sister. "Anyway… Back to business. Why the summons tonight? What's going on?"

Kylie gives me another suspicious look before shaking her head. "Right. I have some news." She pulls out a sheet of paper and slides it across the table, a grin breaking over her face. "We're in the top three!"

She does a weird little shoulder dance while I peruse the email from City Hall—congratulations, stiff competition, fifteen well-qualified entrants, expected final decision within the next few weeks.

Jake's eyes bounce back and forth between Kylie and me. "Congrats?"

"Maybe. We'll see."

Kylie huffs at my lack of excitement. "Oh, come on. Sometimes you've gotta celebrate the small stuff."

I breathe through the pinch in my chest, memories overtaking my previous annoyance as she echoes one of Dad's favorite sayings.

"Plus," she continues, "we should probably celebrate the fact that our favorite mechanic is a step closer to having two good legs."

"I will definitely drink to that," Jake says.

"Good." Kylie stands. "First round's on me. Jake, what do you want?"

Jake's eyes dart to me before he turns his attention to the drink menu. "Oat IPA. Thanks."

Kylie nods. "Be back in a jiff. I'm gonna order some apps, too."

A slow grin spreads across his face, and he nudges my leg with his when Kylie's out of earshot. "So... Best kiss ever, huh?"

"Shut up." I smack his arm.

"Hey. We're allowed to kiss. I signed your paper."

"I know. But I still feel weird about it."

He cocks an eyebrow. "Well then, maybe we need to practice some more."

"Hmm... They do say practice makes perfect."

"Yes, they do. And as an athlete, I support that saying one hundred percent."

The suggestion in his tone sends ripples of anticipation along my nerves. Thank God Kylie slides a beer in front of him and takes a seat. Not sure how much longer I would've lasted with just the two of us.

"Alright," she says. "Care to make tonight interesting?"

Jake's gaze follows Mullet Mike and his rhinestone jumpsuit as he makes his way onstage. "Uh, I think that's taken care of."

I raise my eyebrows at Kylie.

"We each perform something. Twenty bucks to whoever gets the loudest crowd response."

Jake glances over the karaoke menu. "We get to pick our own song?"

"Yep."

He nods. "I'll take that action."

"Me, too."

"Good." Kylie holds up her drink, and we clink glasses. "Eat my dust, suckers."

"Wow," Jake says, his voice low. "Your sister is, uh…"

"I believe the word you're looking for is tone-deaf." We both cringe as she butchers yet another few notes of Journey's *Don't Stop Believin'*.

"You said it. I didn't." Jake tilts his beer to his lips. "But A for effort."

More like D for Delusional. Frankly, I'm surprised they haven't taken the song off the menu. It's like she's proclaimed it to be her own personal Everest. Something she will conquer before she dies.

Which would probably be fairly soon if it were in any other karaoke bar. The patrons that frequent this place are too nice to do anything other than offer support and encouragement, however. Part of the reason why I like it here. No one's gonna get booed off the stage. Although sometimes I do wish they had a gong.

True to form, Kylie garners a healthy smattering of applause when she's done. Plopping down at the table, she takes a swig of her beer and nods at me with a wink. "Alright, sis, get up there and show us what you've got."

What I've got is a case of nervous butterflies.

It usually doesn't bother me too much when I'm up here singing, but Jake's not usually in the audience, either. Looking at me with those warm chocolate eyes, his tongue skimming along his bottom lip. Making my skin flush as I remember his lips on mine, his hands running through my hair. Thinking about what we might do next time we get together…

Dammit, Lauren, focus! You've got a song to sing and twenty bucks to win.

Not that I'm anywhere near as competitive as Kylie, but God forbid she beats me in a singing competition. I'd never live it down.

I close my eyes when the opening strains of *Black Velvet* ooze through the sound system, channeling the sultry essence of Alannah Myles. Calm washes over me as I follow the bouncing ball on the screen, the melody acting as a lullaby to soothe the riotous butterflies.

As long as I don't look at Jake.

Because every time my eyes slingshot back to him, electricity dances down my spine and jolts those damn butterflies back to life.

Somehow, I keep myself together long enough to make it through the song, the trifecta of applause, whistles, and catcalls showing the crowd's appreciation as the final notes fade away.

Kylie gives me a high-five as I take a seat, and she grins at Jake. "Top that, sucker."

"Wow, Lauren." Jake gives a nod of approval. "That was amazing."

"Thanks."

Jake rolls his shoulders and blows out a breath. "Showtime."

"Any idea if he can sing or not?" Kylie asks as Jake takes the stage.

"Nope." But I can't wait to get a chance to sit here and stare at him.

And neither can the majority of the women in the bar, if the excited murmurings are anything to go by. The Blue Hair Ladies are already fanning themselves, and Jake hasn't even opened his mouth yet.

Settling himself onto a high wooden stool, Jake pics up the microphone. A cocky smile tilts his lips, and he winks.

Kylie groans as the opening techy beats of Justin Timberlake's *SexyBack* pulse through the speakers. "Aw, crap."

Less than a minute in, and Jake's already got the catcalls and whistles checked off. Even though he's limited in his movement, he's making full use of what he's got. And what he's got is bucketloads of confidence, a smooth voice, and a good sense of rhythm.

The bicep flexing and teasing glimpses of his abs aren't hurting, either.

"Take it off!" shouts one of the Blue Hair Ladies, waving a couple of dollar bills in the air.

"Ooh—he's fighting dirty." Kylie takes a pull of her beer, her attention locked on Jake. "Is it wrong that I'm kinda turned on right now?"

"Join the club," I mutter.

Kylie's eyes dart to me.

"I mean, clearly, he's a crowd-pleaser."

"Yeah." She turns her attention back to the stage. "We're definitely not using him to his full potential. Oh, speaking of... Have you two gotten together yet?"

I cough in an effort to dislodge my wine from my windpipe. "What?"

"You know... That training session thing you guys were talking about."

"Oh. Yeah. That. Yes, we, uh...did that."

"So? How was it?"

"It was awesome." Crap. That came out breathier than I'd intended.

Kylie gives me a curious look. "Really? Wow. I guess if he can make you rave about bike how-to's, he's a really good teacher."

I clamp my lips shut, not trusting myself to either confirm or deny her words. Plus, there's the whole issue of my brain cells going on strike while Jake continues to work the crowd. Damn. I wonder what he's like when he's *not* in a cast. I wrap my hands around my wineglass to prevent them from fanning myself.

"I think we've been had," Kylie says, begrudgingly adding to the applause at the end of Jake's performance.

Yeah. But what a way to go.

CHAPTER SIXTEEN

Jake

Kylie plucks her keys from the table. "As much as I hate to, I think I need to get going. I'm leading the sunrise trail ride in the morning. You need a ride, Jake?"

"I can take him home." Lauren's cheeks pinken. "It's on my way."

Oh, hot damn. Maybe we'll get a chance to pick up where we left off the other night.

"Alright. See you guys tomorrow." Kylie stands up. "And Jake? If the Motocross thing doesn't work out, I think you've got a second career in strip karaoke."

The excitement at some more alone time with Lauren bottoms out with Kylie's words.

Lauren's brow furrows as she studies me. "You okay?"

"Yeah. I'm fine."

"Liar." She presses her lips together. "What's wrong?" Her eyes widen, and she checks to make sure Kylie's gone. "Oh, shoot. Did I read this wrong? Did you not want me to take you home?"

"No. I mean, yes. Shit. I mean, no, you didn't read it wrong, and yes, I'm glad you're taking me home." I take a deep breath, trying to loosen some of the dread squeezing my chest. "It's just what Kylie said about Motocross not working out. The doc mentioned retirement today at my appointment."

"Oh, Jake." Lauren's eyes fill with empathy, and she reaches out and squeezes my hand. "I'm sorry."

"Yeah. Me, too." Flipping my hand, I twine my fingers with hers, her touch a welcome comfort.

"Do you know what you're gonna do yet?"

"No. It's just…" I run my thumb along hers and sigh. "I don't know. I mean, I love racing. But there's a very real chance that I could throw myself into training after I'm all healed up and still not make it back onto the tour." My gut clenches. "I don't want to be a quitter. But I also don't want to be stupid."

Lauren glances at our hands, her gaze rocketing around the bar as she untangles our fingers. "Sorry," she winces. "Just, uh…too many eyes here, you know?"

"Yeah. I guess." While part of me gets where she's coming from, a tiny part of me is beginning to wonder if it's more than just the employer-employee thing. Like maybe she's ashamed. Shit.

Trapping her lower lip between her teeth, Lauren studies me. "Do you wanna get out of here?"

A spark of hope ignites. "Maybe. What'd you have in mind?"

"Do you trust me?"

"Yeah."

She tugs my hand. "Come on."

Several minutes later, Lauren pulls into an empty parking lot on the college campus.

Maybe that whole trust thing was unfounded after all. "Uh… If you're trying to get me interested in night school, no thanks."

She grins. "Nope." She gets out of the car and waits while I extract myself. "Follow me." She leads us to one corner of the lot and swipes an ID card at a closed gate. "This is the Baker-Williams Arboretum. It closes to the public at dusk, but employees get extended access."

The gate opens with a soft click, and she holds it open for me, then lets it snick shut. Crickets serenade us as we follow a paved footpath through a grove of trees. Our way is lit by tall, old-fashioned, evenly-spaced lamps, and an unusually bright almost-full moon. "Wow. Nice."

"Oh, just wait," she says. "It gets better."

As we round a bend in the path, a large pond comes into view. Cattails ring the edge, and a cluster of water lilies floats nearby.

Lauren sighs. "I love this place. Mom used to bring me here. It's where I come when I need to think." She walks to a bench along the water's edge and sits down, patting the seat next to her. "It's just so peaceful." Closing her eyes, she takes a deep breath.

Yeah. Peaceful and much less populated than the bar. On the other side of the pond, several couples are ambling hand-in-hand, and a few walkers are exercising along various pathways.

Settled beside her, the questions and negative thoughts recede. My blood begins the journey below the belt as I watch Lauren, her chest rising and falling, her lips pursed as she blows out a breath. She rolls her neck from side to side, and my eyes catch on soft skin that's begging for exploration.

Shit. I shift to relieve the increasing pressure in my groin. Is she *trying* to kill me?

"So? Is it helping?" she asks, cracking open an eyelid.

Not in the least.

"Because if not," she continues, "there's always the Pro and Con list."

"Pro and Con list?" What the hell is she talking about? Us?

"Yeah." She angles herself toward me. "What do you most like about Motocross?"

Oh, right. Motocross. I give my head a slight shake in an attempt to clear the lust-goggles and adjust my position to mirror hers, resting my arm along the back of the bench. Hmm… What do I like about Motocross? "Speed. Freedom. The camaraderie."

She nods. "Okay. And what do you like least?"

"Losing."

Lauren rolls her eyes. "Duh. Dig deeper."

"What if I don't have deeper?"

She tilts her head and gives me a knowing smile. "You do."

"Geez. As if having a shrink for a sister isn't bad enough…" I heave an exaggerated sigh. "Fine. Sometimes the lifestyle gets old."

Lauren gives me a questioning look.

"Moving around all the time is fun for a while. But then all the towns start to look the same—same motels, same bars." Same women. "As much as it sucks to rely so much on Tracy and Craig, it's been kind of nice to be in one place." I probably haven't had this stable of a living arrangement since before I left home.

"Good. What else?"

"Giving up." The words claw their way out before I can stop them. "I feel like if I don't at least try to come back, then I'm letting Mom down."

Lauren lays her hand on mine. "Because?"

I swallow past the tightness in my throat. "Because she was big on never giving up. With school and my dyslexia stuff and with herself. There were times she was working three jobs just to make ends meet, but she always kept going."

"Wow. That's a lot to live up to."

She swipes her thumb back and forth across my wrist, and I huff a laugh. "Yeah. Tell me about it. Then there's the whole 'my sister's a psychologist' thing. At least I was the semi-famous athlete. What the hell am I if I'm not a Motocross racer?"

"You're Jake. The adorable, funny guy who is a damn good mechanic, and one hell of a karaoke singer."

Her words loosen the knot in my throat. "Well, someone's gotta bring sexy back."

"You definitely did a good job of that." Her hand stills on my wrist, and she gulps.

"Oh, yeah?" I lock my gaze on hers, my blood heating again at the desire in her eyes. "You weren't too bad yourself."

"Thanks." Lauren's tongue darts out and traces a lazy trail along her lips.

Dammit. She *is* trying to kill me. Oh, hell. If I'm going down, I'm taking her with me. I scoot closer and twine my fingers through her hair. Drawing her toward me, I crush my lips to hers as if it's the only thing keeping me alive.

Surprise flickers over her face, but after only the slightest of hesitations she reciprocates, and we pick up where we left off the other night. The purr of satisfaction in her throat makes my groin tighten even more.

Trying to eliminate any remaining space between us, I shift, and pain ignites in my ankle at the accidental pressure of my foot on the ground. Breaking our liplock, I suck in a breath. "Ow. Dammit!"

Lauren blinks owl eyes of confusion. "What? What happened?"

"Ankle." My knuckles whiten around the edges of the bench as I breathe through the pain. "Fuck."

She winces in sympathy and rubs my back. "Better?" she asks when I blow out another long breath and release my death grip on the bench.

"Maybe?" I shake my head and huff a sarcastic laugh. "Unless you count the fact that I'm now two for two when it comes to killing the mood."

She wrinkles her nose. "Probably for the best. This *is* a public place, after all. Plus, we were supposed to be thinking. Not…doing *that*."

"Yeah, but doing *that* is a lot more fun."

Lauren's brow lowers as she scowls. "Be serious."

"I *am* serious." I lean forward and steal another kiss, then sit back and pull her closer, tucking her to my side. "And thank you. That was very helpful. Both the talking and the kissing."

"Glad to help."

She snuggles closer, and I wrap my arms around her. Damn. I'm not usually a snuggler, but this is kinda nice. Her curves nestled against me. The scent of vanilla mixing with the smells of nature. Quiet companionship without the weight of expectations.

"Tell me about these." She traces the ink on my forearms, little zings of pleasure following her path.

"What do you want to know?"

"How long did they take?"

"A couple of years. Each."

"Really?"

"Yeah. I had to do them piecemeal because of how big they are and because of our schedules and all the travel."

"They're amazing."

"Yeah. Gunther's kind of a legend. When I started out on tour, I was a blank canvas. I'd stop in and see him whenever I was within a few hours' drive."

"What do they mean?"

"Well, this one—" I lift the arm she's tracing "— the dragon, is for luck and strength. Plus, he's a badass." Gunther's work never ceases to amaze me. And Lauren hasn't even gotten the full impact yet.

"He sure is." She taps my other arm. "And this one?"

"That's my guardian angel. She watches over me and tries to prevent me from being a dumbass. She really has her work cut out for her."

"Well, she's spectacular."

"Thanks. You don't happen to have any ink hiding under that good girl exterior, do you?"

"Nope. Not that I'm opposed to it, I just don't know of anything interesting enough."

"Oh, I could totally see you with some ink. Maybe a nice Pro and Con list. Or a tasteful so-ko-du puzzle."

"Sudoku," she says, elbowing me in the ribs with a laugh. "And definitely not."

"Well, I'll keep my eye out for something inspiring."

"You do that."

"Will do. Hey." I tighten my arm, giving Lauren a light squeeze. "Speaking of inspiring, Kylie's news was pretty great, right?"

Her chest expands, her shoulders rising and falling with her sigh. "Yeah. I guess."

"Somehow I'm getting the feeling you don't share your sister's sentiments."

She shrugs. "Well, it's great that we're in the final three and all, but that still only gives us a thirty-three percent chance of getting picked." Tension creeps into her muscles. "The shop should be good for a while yet, but there's a big loan payment due in a few months, and if we can't pay it off, I'm not sure if the bank will refinance it."

"Shit."

"Yeah."

"What would you do?"

Lauren shrugs again. "Not sure. I mean, I'm fine. I can always go back to working full-time here at the school. But as for the shop? Who knows? It'd probably kill Kylie."

And me.

The thought takes me by surprise. I mean, I don't even have any stakes in the business. Hell—I'm not even sure if I'll be around in a year. Although, the more I think about it, the more I find I might not mind. Having one place to call home. One bed to sleep in night after night.

One woman to curl up with.

I stiffen, trying to figure out where *that* thought came from.

"You okay?" Lauren twists and studies me in the moonlight.

"What? Yeah." If you don't count the fact that my subconscious is leaking like a cracked gasket. What the hell is this girl doing to me?

And better yet, why the hell am I not more freaked out about it?

CHAPTER SEVENTEEN

Lauren

I stab the delete button yet again. Damn Excel spreadsheet. It's been giving me nothing but grief this morning. Although if I'm honest, it's probably not the spreadsheet's fault.

No, that honor would go to the riot of confusion swirling through my head. Trying to figure out what I really feel for Jake. I mean, he's so far outside of who I usually go for. Sure he's hot and funny and I like spending time with him, but is it just exciting because we're trying to keep it a secret? Am I simply scratching an itch I didn't know I had? Is he? And how much longer can we keep this up before Kylie finds out? More to the point—do I even care anymore?

My brain's busy weighing the pros and cons of telling her versus continuing to keep things a secret. Of course, there really isn't anything to tell. So far, we've only kissed. Granted, they were very good kisses. Like, the panty-melting, I-forgot-where-I-was-for-a-minute kisses, but still. Maybe if things keep progressing, *then* I'll consider telling her.

Although, that's weird, too. I don't tell her when I sleep with my other boyfriends. So maybe in this case ignorance really *is* bliss.

Wait. Is Jake my boyfriend? We've only kissed a couple of times. And we haven't even really been out on a date. Okay, maybe dinner after Pedals & Medals could be construed as date-adjacent, but I really think that was more of a weird circumstance. And then there was last night after karaoke. The arboretum's certainly scenic enough for a date spot. But I totally wasn't thinking about it when I took him there. I really was only trying to help.

And we definitely haven't had The Talk yet. Do people even have The Talk at our age? And if we do have The Talk, will it scare him off? I kind of like what we have now, even if it is less defined than what I typically aspire to.

Plus, he has enough on his plate right now. As confused as I am about things, I think he has it ten times worse—having to figure out if he's going to continue with his career or hang it up.

My chest tightens.

Last night I told Jake I'd be fine if things don't work out with the shop. But ever since then, I've been reconsidering my answer. Because I don't think I would be. Financially, yes, I'd be fine. But the more I think about it, the more I'd probably feel like Jake—like I was letting Dad down. Not to mention Gramps. Geez. We'd be third-generation let downs. Great.

It's times like these I kind of wish I was more like Kylie. Able to stay upbeat and believe that things will work out. But I'm not. And maybe that's for the best. Someone's got to be the voice of reason.

I just wish it didn't have to me all the time.

The invitation to Aunt Sheila's and Uncle Pete's for dinner really could not have come at a better time. For all of us.

The edge in Aunt Sheila's voice when she called this afternoon had me questioning just how big of a wine bottle to bring tonight. By the look of desperation in her eyes when she opens the door, I'd say my choice of the jumbo size was the right one.

"Girls! Come in!" She envelops each of us in a hug and then ushers us inside. "Bless you, my child," she says, eyeballing the wine.

Kylie trails behind me and sets the six-pack of a local brew on the kitchen island. She and Uncle Pete always bond over beers while Aunt Sheila and I go for the grapes.

"You really didn't have to do this, Aunt Sheila," I say. "We could've brought something."

Aunt Sheila waves my words away. "It's my pleasure. You two work hard. You deserve a home-cooked meal every now and then. Plus—" she jabs a corkscrew into the wine bottle "—it kept me from murdering your uncle."

Kylie winces. "That bad, huh?"

Aunt Sheila pours two glasses, hands one to me, then takes a long gulp. "Let's just say that if he ever fully retires, I think I'm gonna have to get a job.

Honestly, I don't know how all those retired couples do it." She takes another slurp. "Did you know he's taken over management of the dishwasher?"

"Oh. Well, at least he's helping out," I say.

Aunt Sheila's fingers tighten around her wine glass. "Sure. If by 'helping' you mean griping about how I load the dishwasher, then grumbling when the dishes come out still dirty. It's because he's not loading the damn thing right! But will he listen to me or let me do it? Noooo. Not like I haven't been doing it for fifty years, but sure. What do I know?"

Kylie and I share a glance, and she asks, "Uh, where *is* Uncle Pete?"

"I banished him to his cave." Sheila brings her fingers to her lips and whistles. "Pete! The girls are here!"

"How is he?" Kylie tilts her head toward Uncle Pete's den.

"You mean besides driving me crazy?" Aunt Sheila rolls her eyes. "He's fine."

"Hey, it's my favorite nieces!" Uncle Pete ambles into the room, one arm in a sling and a big grin on his whiskered face. The fact that we're his only nieces never stops him from referring to us like this.

Kylie gives him a side-arm hug, careful to avoid his sling. "So, when are you coming back, old man?"

"Not soon enough," Aunt Sheila mutters.

Uncle Pete scowls at her, then turns to Kylie. "Doc says one more week of home arrest and then I can come cause trouble at the shop."

"As long as you're causing trouble one-handed." Aunt Sheila pins him with a knowing look before looking at us. "Seriously. You guys might want to install cameras. Make sure he's not taking off his sling. 'Cause I am *not* going through this again." She shakes her head. "You know how sometimes I used to say I wanted kids? Well, now I have one."

"Hey. I'm standing right here," Uncle Pete says.

"Yes, you are." Aunt Sheila sighs. "All. The damn. Time."

"Ookay…" Kylie glances between our aunt and uncle, and I can tell we're both trying to figure out how to avert World War Three. "So, who wants to hear about Lauren's secret lover?"

The bickering screeches to a halt as two silver-streaked heads swivel my direction. My face heats, and I send Kylie silent death threats. Not quite the diversion I had in mind.

Kylie shrugs, her expression a mixture of "sorry to throw you under the bus" and "I didn't know what else to do."

The silence cracks open as Aunt Sheila rapid-fires questions. "What? Who? Spill!"

Uncle Pete sniffs, the scent of pot roast hanging heavy in the air. "Any chance we can discuss this over dinner?"

"Pete!" Aunt Sheila barks. "There are more important matters than your stomach."

"Right." I nod, finally finding my voice. "Like clearing up the fact that I do *not* have a lover."

The disappointment on Aunt Sheila's face might be comical if I wasn't on the receiving end of it. "Damn. And here I was hoping to live vicariously through you."

"Again!" Uncle Pete throws up his good arm. "I'm right here."

Aunt Sheila rolls her eyes again, then turns her attention to herding us into the dining room.

Following a few tense moments wondering if something other than the roast beef might end up getting stabbed, things settle into our normal routine. Uncle Pete and Kylie always wind up talking sports, while Aunt Sheila and I talk books and movies, with shop-talk all-inclusive.

As Kylie fills them in on the proposal, I get that unsettled feeling once again. I wait until after we've clinked glasses in celebration, then throw in the two cents that've been giving me pause. "Okay. So, I know being in the final three for this is a big deal, but I still think we need to talk about what happens if we don't get it."

Kylie's eyes go wide. "Why? Is there something you're not telling me? Did you find something in the books?"

"No. Nothing like that. It's just..." I drive a piece of pot roast through my mashed potatoes. "We know Dad's life insurance money will be coming soon. But we also know it wasn't the top of the line, so it won't be as much help as we were hoping. We've had a good spring so far, and the classes and one-on-ones Jake's putting together should help, too. And I want to believe we'll win the proposal just as much as you, but I think we have to plan for both possibilities. What we'll do if we get it, and what we'll do if we don't."

Relief settles on Kylie's features. "Phew. You had me worried, there." Her eyebrows draw together in inquiry. "How are the numbers?"

"Good. For now. It's that balloon payment I'm worried about. I just don't see us being able to manage it if things remain status quo."

"We can always go back to the bank and refinance it."

"Yeah. Maybe. But what if they *don't* refinance it? What then?"

Kylie sighs and sinks her head into her hands, her elbows propped on the table. "I don't know." She gulps a breath, her voice wavering as she continues. "It wasn't supposed to be like this."

Shit. And now I've made my sister cry. Great job, Lauren.

Aunt Sheila and I stand up and surround Kylie, pulling her into a hug, while Uncle Pete looks like he'd rather be somewhere else. Somewhere without estrogen and emotions.

Kylie sucks in a breath, and I can tell she's trying her best to keep it together. She hates crying just about as much as Uncle Pete hates to be around people with leaky tear ducts. "I'm scared, too," she whispers. With a deep breath, she nods, then pulls away, and we all take our seats again. "But I have to believe things will be okay. It's too overwhelming otherwise."

Hmm. I totally get that. But I also get that there's a fine line between optimism and delusion. And I don't want us ending up on the wrong side.

"You know—" Aunt Sheila reaches across the table, placing a hand on each of ours "—this is exactly why your father left the shop to both of you. Because you balance each other out."

She squeezes our hands, and Uncle Pete clears his throat. "And, um, no matter what happens, your dad would be real proud of you. Both of you."

By the convulsive swallowing and the tick of Kylie's jaw, I'd say Uncle Pete's words are hitting her just about as hard as they're hitting me. For someone who likes to avoid the "touchy-feely crap" as he usually calls it, he sure pressed the right button.

Kylie clears her throat. "Thanks."

I nod, still battling the emotions lodged firmly in my throat.

"Anytime." Aunt Sheila squeezes our hands again, then lets go. She winks at Uncle Pete, her features softened. "Now. Who wants pie?"

After dessert, Kylie and Uncle Pete head to the Man Cave while Aunt Sheila and I have another glass of wine in the kitchen. It's as much because Kylie and I are trying to give our aunt and uncle some breathing room from each other as because that's just how it usually pans out—me chatting with Aunt Sheila and Kylie watching sports with Uncle Pete.

Aunt Sheila gives me a shoulder squeeze. "You okay?"

I nod. "I could ask you the same thing."

She shakes her head, a wry grin on her face. "Yeah, I'm fine. Ready for him to get back to work and out of the house, but fine." She gives me a pointed look.

"Yeah. I'm fine, too. It's not like I'm lying awake all night thinking about the shop. I just…" I sigh. "I don't want to let Dad down."

"Oh, honey. There is nothing you could do that would let him down. You know that, right?"

I shrug, the emotions clogging my throat once again.

"Your father loved you both so much. Whatever happens with the shop won't change that. It's just a business." Aunt Sheila sips her wine and continues her knowing stare until I nod. "Good. Now that that's taken care of, let's circle back to that whole 'secret lover' thing." She wiggles her eyebrows, a smile playing at her lips.

I groan. "Do we have to?"

"Yes. Inquiring minds want to know."

"Do inquiring minds promise to keep their lips sealed?"

As Mom's younger sister, Aunt Sheila has always been a good sounding board. And it's killing me not to be able to confide in anyone right now. I mean, what good is panty-melting kissing if you can't brag about it? Plus, I could really use an outside perspective right now. But how much do I tell her?

Aunt Sheila locks her lips and throws the key over her shoulder, her eyes bright with excitement.

"So… It's not so much a secret lover as a secret kisser."

"Do you want it to be more?"

"Yes." The word explodes out of my mouth.

Aunt Sheila grins. "Alrighty, then. Tell me how you really feel."

"Ugh. That's just it. I don't know how I feel. I mean, I really like him, but he's so far out of my league it's not even funny." Even though I'm less intimidated by him than when we first met, that fact's still true. "And I don't know if we're just having fun, or if we're headed for something more."

"No one does. Unfortunately, things like this don't fit nicely into spreadsheets."

"Ugh, I know." Life would be so much easier if they did.

"Are you gonna tell me who it is? Do I know him?"

I weigh out the pros and cons, finally deciding to let her in on my secret. "It's Jake. Our new mechanic." I brace for warnings, but instead, excitement lights her eyes. "Ooh… Good choice. If I were twenty years younger and single, I'd go all dreamy-eyed over him, too."

Yeah. You and every other female. "So? What do I do?"

"Well, I could tell you to be careful. That he's got 'heartbreaker' written all over him." She tilts her head to the side and studies me. "But sometimes you've just gotta relax, let go, and enjoy the ride."

Right. Easy for her to say.

CHAPTER EIGHTEEN

Jake

What the hell am I doing?

I mean, I know what I'm doing *right now*—replacing the tires on a couple of the shop's rental bikes. Unfortunately, there isn't anything more complicated that needs fixing right now. Which means that my thoughts keep ricocheting back to Lauren and what the hell *we're* doing.

Are we just kissing friends? Kissing coworkers? Friends with mediocre benefits? Okay. Maybe more than mediocre. The kisses have been spectacular. But they make me want more.

The problem is, do I deserve more?

I feel like I'm totally out of my element here. Because I like her. I *really* like her. But I don't want to hurt her. And I'm afraid if we go any further, that's exactly what I'll do. One, because I'm not exactly stable boyfriend material, and two... Well, that's pretty much it—I'm not exactly stable boyfriend material. Which is what she deserves.

Shit.

When did I start to grow a conscience?

"Uncle Jake!"

Reece's excited yell and the thudding of his steps breaks through the tangle in my brain.

Thank God. Saved by my nephew.

Reece appears in the doorway, Tracy right behind him. "Sorry," she says, a wince on her face. "Hope this is an okay time to stop by."

"It's perfect. Hey, Reece's Pieces."

"Hi!" Reece skips into the room and stops beside me. "What are you doing?"

"Working."

"Duh." He rolls his eyes. "I *know* that."

"Oh. My mistake," I say, straight-faced. "Well, if you *must* know, right now, I'm about to put new tires on this bike. You wanna help?"

"Can I, Mom?"

"Sure. Knock yourself out."

I glance up at Tracy. "If you, uh, need to go run some errands, we're fine." I know how much work Reece can be, and my sister could probably use a few moments to herself.

"Really?" Tracy's face lights up. "Are you sure?"

"Yeah. I've got this."

"Okay. I'll be back soon. Be good for your uncle."

"No sweat, Mom!"

Thank God the kid's curious. His steady stream of questions keeps my mind off my personal life as I teach him the ins and outs of basic tire care.

"Hey, Jake? Can you—" Lauren stops in the doorway, surprise on her face. "Oh. Hi. Kylie didn't tell me you had company back here."

"I'm not company. I'm his nephew! Reece!"

"Hi, Reece. I'm Lauren."

Reece hops from one foot to the other. "Are you Uncle Jake's boss?"

"One of them, yes."

He tilts his head to the side. "Do you like my Uncle Jake?"

"Uh…" Her cheeks flush, and her eyes dart to mine before settling back on Reece. "He's a very good employee, yes."

"Well, I like my Uncle Jake. He's fun. Do you know he rides bikes?"

Lauren nods. "I heard something like that."

"But he can't right now, 'cause he messed up his leg. But that's okay, 'cause now he gets to hang out with me. And you know what else? He even let me pick out the colors for his casts."

"He did, huh?"

"Yep. His first one was green for the Hulk. And this one's blue. But I couldn't decide if it was for Batman or Superman. Batman's got blue legs, and Superman's mostly blue with red legs. So I guess it's kinda both."

Lauren bites back a smile as she catches my eye. "Your uncle sounds like a pretty cool guy."

Reece's cowlick waves as he nods. "Uh-huh. He is. You know what else is cool?"

"What?" Lauren asks.

"His penis does tricks!"

Damn. And this had been going so well. "Oh, hey, Reece, buddy." I pull him toward me, one hand clamped over his mouth. "Remember what your mom said?"

Reece's gives me a mournful look. "No penis talk in public," he mumbles through my fingers.

"Yep."

"Okay." He heaves a sigh twice his size, then turns back to Lauren. "I'm not supposed to talk about penises in public, because Mom says so. She also tells me to keep my hands out of my pants."

Lauren presses her lips together as she struggles to maintain her composure. "Well, I'd say that's some pretty good advice."

"Hey, Reece," I interject. "Why don't you tell Lauren what else you like to do?" Besides embarrass me and play with yourself. "What'd we do last night?"

"Oh! We played dinosaurs. And cars. Do you drive a car?" he asks Lauren.

"Yep."

"Me too. When I get bigger. And you know what else I'm gonna do when I get big? Ride with Uncle Jake. He has a cool bike." He tilts his head and studies Lauren. "You're big. Do you ride with Uncle Jake on his cool bike?"

Glancing at Lauren, my blood makes a detour to my groin as she licks her lips, a faint blush highlighting her cheekbones. I wonder if she's picturing what I am—her behind me on a motorcycle, her arms locked around my waist, her softness molded against my body. I shift to relieve some of the pressure building below my waist and clear my throat. "You ever ride a motorcycle?"

"No."

"Do we need to add that to the list?"

She nods. "Definitely."

An idea begins to filter through my brain cells. Damn. I think my penis-obsessed, four-year-old nephew might just be a genius.

CHAPTER NINETEEN

Lauren

"I still can't believe I let you kidnap me."

Jake barks out a laugh from my passenger's seat. "Kidnap? Please. You're driving."

"Yeah, but under extreme duress."

"Duress. Right. You practically jumped into the car."

Argh! He's right. I did. But in my defense, I underwent a healthy dose of second-guessing beforehand. And I still can't quite believe I'm doing it. Not that I actually know what *it* is. Or where we're headed. Or why I agreed.

Okay. I know *why* I agreed. It's because of the hot guy in the seat next to me. Well, that and the fact that he said it was part of my homework. How can I say no to homework? Especially in light of Aunt Sheila's "sit back and enjoy the ride" comment. Of course, it'd be much easier if I knew where the ride was taking me.

All I know is that Jake asked if I could take off a couple of days, told me to pack an overnight bag, and then refused to answer any of my questions other than "bring comfortable clothes" and "don't overthink it."

Yeah, right. Has he met me? I've done nothing *but* overthink it.

Is Kylie gonna figure out that I'm not really busy with end-of-quarter stuff at the college? Does Jake really have an appointment with a specialist, or is that just his cover story? Can I trust Aunt Sheila to keep her mouth shut while she and Uncle Pete are helping out at the store? Does this mean Jake and I are dating? Should I have packed sexier? Did I underpack?

Or maybe I overpacked. Maybe we'll spend a couple of days naked in a love shack somewhere.

A giddy warmth spreads through my core. Yeah. I could definitely handle that.

Unless we're naked with other people. Didn't he say his mother worked at a nudist colony?

The giddy warmth is replaced by a ball of dread. "Are you taking me to meet your mother?"

"What? No." Jake shifts in his seat. "Would you please relax? This is supposed to be fun."

"Well, I *would* relax if you told me where we're going."

He pulls out his phone. "Don't make me call Sheila."

I growl a retort. Damn Aunt Sheila for being so willing to help me play hooky, and damn my own big, fat mouth for telling *him* about it. She'd probably shoot me full of tranquilizers and drive me to wherever-the-hell-it-is-we're-going by herself if she had to. "Just one little hint."

"Sorry." Jake cranks up the music. "I can't hear you."

I open my mouth to continue arguing, but close it when he starts singing along with Imagine Dragon's *Demons*. Damn. I love this song. And a good car singalong. Add Jake to the mix, and it's a perfect trifecta. His voice is a curious blend of sedative and stimulant. On the one hand, his smooth, sexy baritone calms my high-flying nerves, but on the other hand, it sends tingles of excitement racing up and down my spine.

Right now, I think I'd be happy if the only thing he had planned was driving around singing car karaoke all day.

The haunting tranquility fades away, and Jake riffs on his air guitar to the opening strains of Aerosmith's *Walk This Way*. "Come on," he says, when Steven Tyler starts singing. "You know you want to."

"I don't know the words."

"Phfft. No one knows the words." He continues to strum his guitar and sings along, his words a mixture of nonsense and actual lyrics.

I join in, and we harmonize on the chorus. Despite the fact that we're both wailing along with the song, we sound pretty good together.

We keep ourselves entertained for quite some time, and before I know it, Jake's directing me off the highway. "Okay. Just follow the signs for the stadium."

"Stadium?"

"Yep. Big, round thing? You can't miss it."

"Gee. Thanks. What I meant was, *why* are we going to the stadium?"

"You'll see."

Hmm... "Did you get us tickets to a baseball game? Or football? Hockey? Which one's in season right now?"

"Well, it's a football stadium, but they're not in season yet, so no."

"Is Cirque du Soleil in town?"

"I have no idea."

"Are we headed for the annual karaoke strip convention?"

"Why? Would you like that?"

"Maybe."

"Then maybe."

"Are you auditioning for *America's Got Talent*?"

"No."

"Am *I* auditioning for *America's Got Talent*?"

He shakes his head, a disgustingly smug smile on his face.

I continue to pepper him with questions, but he continues to evade anything resembling an answer. Dammit. Why is this turning me on? I thrive on the known. But I guess if I'm honest, there's something freeing about letting Jake take over. It's kind of exciting.

As we get closer to our destination, however, something in the air seems to shift. Jake's good leg bounces like it's on a spring, and every time I glance his way, it seems that the tension in his shoulders has ratcheted up another few notches.

"Shit," he breathes as I turn into the stadium parking lot. "This was a stupid idea. Maybe we should just turn around and go back home."

"What? And miss The Wiggles Live in Concert? Dora the Explorer on Ice? Don't make me call Aunt Sheila."

The corner of his mouth twitches. "Please. Give me a little credit. If it was The Wiggles or Dora, Reece would be in the backseat." He takes a breath and rakes a hand through his hair. "I actually got us Supercross tickets. There's an event today, and my buddy Hurley's competing. I thought it would be fun—play hooky, get that motorcycle ride you wanted. You know... Put a couple of notches in your bad girl column. But, uh, we don't actually have to go. We can find something else to do. Something classier."

His insecurity tugs at my heartstrings. I pull into a parking space, then shift to face him. "Are you kidding me? This is awesome." Never in a million years would I have guessed this is what we'd be doing. And never in a million years would I have thought I'd actually be this excited about it. But I am. Partly because it's so far out of my typical norm, and partly because it's spending a day with Jake. And, apparently, the night.

Butterflies beat an erratic rhythm in my stomach.

"Uh-oh," Jake says. "That's your thinking face. Are you having second thoughts about how awesome my plan is?"

"Absolutely not." I've never loved a plan more.

"Welcome to my world." Jake balances on his crutches and spreads out his arms as we enter the inner sanctum of the stadium.

I look around in awe. The immense area that's usually a field or concert venue has been turned into a gigantic dirt track. Several motorcycles soar through the air, the buzzing whine of the engines a mechanical harmony to their acrobatics. Small crowds of people mill around the edges, some on the giving end of autographs, some on the receiving end, while others gather around sponsor tents.

"Wow."

Jake grins. "I know. Right?" His previous apprehension seems to have disappeared, and excitement sparkles in his eyes.

"This is your world?"

"Yeah. Kind of. I usually ride outdoors, but there were no Motocross events nearby, and Supercross is more spectator friendly." He nods toward one of the riders signing autographs. "That's Hurley. Come on. Let me introduce you."

A guy around our age wearing a hat and a racing uniform finishes signing a racing glove for a young boy, then looks up. The corners of his eyes crinkle when he sees us. "Dude! You made it."

Jake stops next to him and gives him a fist bump. "Hey, man. Good to see you again."

The boy does a double-take, his eyes rounding. "Are you Jake Chambers? Can I have your autograph, too?"

"Absolutely." Jake grins and signs the boy's hat.

"How's your leg?" the boy asks. "Will you be back next year?"

"It's getting better. I'll try my best. Thanks for asking." Jake takes the questions in stride, showing no signs of the self-doubt he's shared over the past few weeks.

After the boy moves on to another booth, Jake introduces me to Hurley.

"Nice to meet you, Lauren. Any friend of Jake's is a friend of mine." Hurley's expression sobers. "Uh… Speaking of *friends*. Incoming." He coughs the last word, then turns to sign another autograph as a set of blonde twins approaches.

"Hi, Jake," one of the bombshells says.

The other reaches out and runs a hand up his bicep. "How are you doing? You coming back soon?"

"Uh… Hey, Astrid. Sigrid."

"We miss you."

"Yeah, um… I miss you too. I mean, racing. Being on tour."

The first bombshell licks her lips. "Well, you should hang with us tonight. We'll take good care of you."

A mixture of jealousy and insecurity courses through my veins. I mean, they're gorgeous. Clearly much more in Jake's league than I am. But come on. I'm right here. Although as far as they know, I could be his cousin.

Shifting uncomfortably, I glance around, looking for the nearest emergency exit. Blonde twin bombshells count as emergencies, right?

Jake blinks, his expression somewhere between discomfort and panic. "Uh, no thanks. I'm here with Lauren. My *girlfriend*."

My eyes snap back to Jake. Did he just call me his girlfriend?

A gooey warmth chases away the insecurity for a brief moment before it returns in full force. Because yes, he did call me that, but did he mean it? Was it for real? Or was he just trying to get the twins off his back? And if it was the last option, why? And what the hell is he doing here with me when he could have *them*?

Bombshell number one rakes me from top to bottom, while bombshell number two shrugs and pats him on the ass. "Well," she says, "you know where to find us."

Crap. Sounds like he probably *has* had them. Which makes the prospect of tonight even *more* daunting.

The twins amble back to one of the tents, and Jake winces. "Sorry. They work for one of my old sponsors."

"They seem...friendly." And limber. And toned.

Hurley barks out a laugh. "Yeah. That's one way of putting it." He rocks back on his heels and grins. "So, I hear you're a virgin."

My eyes dart to Jake. "Uh..."

"A motorcycle virgin," Jake clarifies.

"Oh. Yeah."

"Well, have no fear. Hurley's here."

Hurley sweeps a gentleman's bow, and Jake rolls his eyes at him before turning to me. "If you're up for it, Hurley's gonna take you for a ride on his bike." He glances at his cast. "Sorry I can't do it. I don't think my leg can handle it."

"His loss is my gain." Hurley winks. "Milady."

"Have fun." Jake narrows his eyes. "But not too much."

If I'm not mistaken, the look on his face is a mixture of disappointment and jealousy. The gooey warm sensation returns, and I plant a kiss on his cheek. "Thank you. This is great. And for the record, I expect a raincheck from you when you're back on your own two feet."

Relief sweeps the uncertainty off his face. "Deal."

CHAPTER TWENTY

Jake

Envy claws at my gut as Lauren hops off the back of Hurley's bike and gives him a hug.

Shit.

On the one hand, I'm excited that she's so excited. I love seeing her so carefree. Especially knowing how much the business stuff is weighing her down. But I don't love seeing her arms wrapped around another guy. Even if that other guy is one of my best friends.

I shake my head, trying to clear the crazy.

Dammit. Since when am I jealous of Hurley? It's usually the other way around. Him busting *my* balls because of my ways with the ladies.

And speaking of ladies… I dart a nervous glance toward the motor oil tent. I seriously hope the twins got the hint. Don't need them messing things up.

"Oh, my God. That was amazing!"

The joy on Lauren's face chases away my misgivings. "Have I created an adrenaline junkie?"

"Absolutely." She wrinkles her nose. "But, uh, at the risk of being un-adrenaline-junkie-ish, where's the restroom? I kinda hafta pee."

Hurley directs her to the nearby VIP restrooms, then crosses his arms, studying me. "Dude. Can I just congratulate you on finally getting your shit together?"

"What?" I'm pretty sure my shit is nowhere in the vicinity of together.

"I like her."

"Yeah. Me, too. Keep your grubby mitts off."

Hurley shakes his head. "My, how the mighty have fallen."

"Shut up, man. It's not like that."

"Oh really?" Hurley cocks an eyebrow. "Well, then, I must've had a stroke a little while ago, because I could've sworn that I heard you call her your girlfriend."

"Oh. Yeah. That. It kinda slipped out."

"Phfft. Only Jake Chambers would accidentally call someone his girlfriend."

"Hey! I panicked. The twins were getting handsy."

"Never bothered you before."

"Yeah, well… Maybe I've changed." Or maybe I wanna change. I tighten my hands around my crutches.

"Dude. What's with you?" Hurley's eyebrows draw together. "You *are* coming back, right?"

I clear my throat, trying to dislodge the ball of fear that's been setting up shop more and more frequently. "I don't know, man. I don't know if I have it in me."

Hurley lets out a low whistle. "Shit, man."

"Yeah."

"What are you gonna do?"

I shrug. "I don't know. I mean, I guess I could always do something with the tour. Or try to hook up with one of the sponsors. Not with the twins, though." I shudder. They take that whole crazy-hot scale to ridiculous levels. And not in a good way. "But I'm kinda liking where I am now." Both at the shop and with Lauren. Thoughts that would've triggered disbelief and more than a little panic several weeks ago.

"Well, I'm sorry to hear I won't be able to bust your balls in person on a regular basis, but I totally get it. And if you *do* decide to come back, you know I'm here for you." He nods his head toward Lauren, who's making her way toward us. "And if you screw it up with her, let me know. I'll happily step in."

"You know these crutches are the only things saving your ass, right?"

"Yep." His grin stretches wide as he tips his hat to Lauren. "Alright guys. It's been a pleasure, but I've gotta go get ready."

"Good luck! And thanks again," says Lauren.

"Yeah. Break a leg. Or two," I mutter.

"Wow," Lauren says, as we make our way to our seats. "I really like him."

Envy claws at me again.

"He's a really nice guy," she adds.

"Uh-huh."

"And I totally see why you do it—the freedom, the speed, the threat of danger. It's just so exhilarating."

"Yep." Although I'm beginning to see the draw toward a slower pace and a little more security.

She stops and lays a hand on my arm. "Thank you."

"You're welcome. I'm glad you had fun with Hurley."

"I did. But what I really wanted was to ride you." Her eyes widen, and a faint blush stains her cheeks. "I mean, *with* you. Ride *with* you. On the seat. Behind you." She groans. "You know what I mean."

"I do." Any remaining irritation falls away, and I chuckle. Damn, I like this girl. Her entertaining faux pas, her willingness to step outside of her box, her shy smile.

After we're settled in our VIP seats, Lauren bites her lip. "So, uh, about that girlfriend comment..." She laces her fingers together and blows out a breath. "I mean, it's cool if you meant it. In fact, I'd like it. But I'm also okay if you were just saying it so those women would leave you alone. Although I'm not quite sure why you'd want them to leave you alone."

"You mean besides the fact that they're crazy?" I drape an arm around Lauren's shoulders. "I really did mean it. I like you. A lot. But I'm not exactly boyfriend material. Especially not for someone like you. So if you don't want to—"

"What do you mean 'someone like me?'"

"You know... Someone smart and real who knows what the hell she's doing in life."

Lauren leans over and plants her lips on mine, stealing any remaining arguments. When we finally come up for air, she rests her forehead against mine. "Shut up. And stop doubting yourself. You're funny and charming and relaxed. Which makes *me* relaxed. Well, not at first. At first you scared the crap out of me. But *now* you relax me. You're the *perfect* boyfriend material for someone like me."

Huh. What do you know? Maybe I am smarter than I thought.

CHAPTER TWENTY-ONE

Lauren

I slide into my car, waiting while Jake tucks himself into the passenger's seat. "Wow. So, we're officially dating now, huh?"

"Yeah. Why? Are you having second thoughts already?"

"What? No. But I am kind of thinking that you set the bar pretty high. I mean, on your first day as my boyfriend, you sort-of-kidnapped me, gave me a thirst for danger, and turned me into a sports fan. Not sure how you're gonna top that."

A wicked smile curves his lips. "Oh, I have an idea or two." His expression sobers. "But I wouldn't want to overdo it. We should probably pace ourselves. I wouldn't want to corrupt you all at once."

"I think I can handle a little more corruption."

"Yeah. We'll just see about that."

Anticipation races through my veins as I follow Jake's directions. My enthusiasm wanes, however, when we arrive at a motel on the outskirts of the city.

The one-story L-shaped structure looks like it's seen better days, and the neon sign proclaiming free Wi-Fi and cable TV fizzles every few seconds.

"It doesn't look like much, but I think you'll like it. Wait here." Jake disappears into the door marked Office, reappearing shortly thereafter. "Okay. We're good. Follow the driveway around the side. We have one of the cottages in back."

Jake unlocks the door and waits like a kid trying to contain his excitement Christmas morning.

"Wow. This is uh…clean." Not quite the love shack I'd been anticipating. More like a shack someone's grandmother lives in. If she was still living in the Fifties. A robin's egg blue loveseat and a mint green armchair congregate around a space-age-style coffee table in one corner of a small living area, atomic starburst curtains line the windows, and a polka-dot carpet covers the floor. A king-size bed covered with a patchwork quilt occupies the far side of the room.

"Trust me." Jake winks. "The best it yet to come. It's been a long day. Why don't you go freshen up and get into something comfy?"

I pause, a hand on my bag. Does he mean comfy sexy? Or comfy sweatpants?

As if reading my mind, he adds, "Something you won't mind getting a bit, uh, dirty."

"Um… If you signed me up for some secret Jell-O wrestling competition, I don't think I'm quite at that level of corruption yet."

Jake licks his lips. "Oh, God. Don't tempt me."

Before I can ask for further clarification on his instructions, someone knocks at the door. "Room service," calls a gruff voice.

Jake crutches to the door and opens it. "Aha! Hey, Bert. Can you put it over there?" Jake gestures toward the table beside the bed. "No peeking," he says to me.

An older man with a beer belly and more hair sprouting from his ears than his head enters the room and sets a plastic take-out container down. "Enjoy."

"Seriously? This place has room service?" I ask after Bert leaves.

"Nope." Jake grins and shakes his head. "It's from the diner next door. Okay. You ready for that next round of corruption?"

I look down at my shirt and jeans. "I honestly have no idea. Should I go change?"

"Nah. You're fine." He sits down on the bed, takes off his shoe, then pulls himself back so he's leaning against the headboard. He pats the empty spot beside him. "Your turn."

Following his lead, I kick off my shoes and sit next to him. Ooh—very comfy. Much better than any hotel mattress I've ever slept on. I think it might be even better than mine. And I *love* my mattress. "Okay. Now what?"

"Now—" he places the plastic container between us and opens it with a flourish "—we eat. In bed." He gasps in faux horror.

Aww. This is sweet. Not quite the hot and spicy I'd been hoping for, but maybe he's planning to work up to that. Although... Is that a hot fudge brownie sundae? Images of my naked Jake dessert fantasy flash through my head, and I gulp.

Jake's eyes sparkle as he dips a finger into the whipped cream mountain, then holds it in front of my lips.

Anticipation flutters in my stomach again. I'm in bed. With Jake. And a hot fudge brownie sundae. "Okay. I think I'm beginning to see the possibilities."

"Thought so."

I flick my tongue out, capturing the dollop off his finger. His eyes darken, and his Adam's apple bobs. Ooh, yeah. I think I'm gonna like it here.

A slow smile curves his lips, and he digs the spoon into the dessert, then wraps his lips around the fudge-drizzled brownie. "Mmm. Damn, that's good. You want some?"

I nod, lust clogging my throat.

He digs his spoon into the gooey fudge again but pauses before offering me a bite. "I don't know. I'd feel kind of bad if you got chocolate on your shirt. Maybe you should take it off."

Oh, that sneaky sonofabitch. He is smooth. "Just to be clear, are you threatening me with dessert?"

"Threatening? No. Hoping to fulfill one of my fantasies right now? Absolutely."

Desire curls in my belly, kinking as I remember what I'm wearing. "Uh, your fantasies don't happen to include a sensible bra and cotton briefs, do they?"

Jake groans. "Now they do." While I'm still contemplating the need to change into something sexier, Jake holds up the spoon.

Sexy underwear? Or take my chances and go with the flow?

Leaning forward, I liberate the brownie from Jake. Wow. That *is* good.

The low moan from my throat makes Jake's eyes flash, and he tugs me toward him, flicking his tongue across the fudgy trail on my lips. "Mmm. Sweet and delicious. Just like you."

Nudging the take-out carton out of the way, he rolls me so I'm straddling his thighs. As he leans back against the headboard, he draws me with him. He nibbles my lower lip, then moves his attention to my jawline while he skims his fingers under my shirt. Excited tingles follow the path of his hands as they slowly work the cotton tee over my head. "Beautiful," he breathes before working his way down my neck again.

Okay. I *love* this plan.

His soft, reverent kisses send shivers racing down my spine.

"Still too many clothes," he murmurs.

"Amen." I tug his T-shirt off, then swipe my finger through the whipped cream. I pause, momentarily mesmerized by his tattoos. The artwork is impressive peeking out from his short sleeves, but absolutely stunning fully exposed. The dragon looks like it's climbing up his arm, its head resting on his shoulder, and the guardian angel keeps watch over the other side, its wings wrapping around his chest and disappearing to his back.

"You like what you see?"

"Definitely. They're gorgeous. And so are you. But I'll bet you taste even better." Holy hell. I do *not* know where that bravado came from. Probably some mixture of hormones and sugar rush. But right now, I don't really care.

I dot his abs with whipped cream, then take my time savoring my handiwork with my tongue. By his hitched breathing, I'd say it's a safe bet Jake's enjoying my bravado as much as I am.

"Okay. My turn." In one swift move, he pops my bra off and rolls us both over. He props himself up on an elbow, then drags a finger through the fudge sauce and draws lazy chocolate abstract art across my chest and around my belly button. A lascivious grin works its way across his lips. "Oops. Looks like I made a mess. I should probably clean that up for you."

I gulp, then shudder as he alternately laps at the chocolate and sucks it off.

Oh. My. God. If this is what corruption feels like, I am never following the rules again.

Satisfaction hums through my veins, and I snuggle closer to Jake.

When Aunt Sheila told me to enjoy the ride, I don't think that was what she had in mind. Although it is Aunt Sheila, so who knows?

What I *do* know is that Jake is fantastic. And I may never move from this spot. Partly because I don't want to, and partly because I'm not actually sure I can.

Jake kept "accidentally" painting me with chocolate, his artwork and subsequent cleanup gradually migrating down my body. Our pants and underwear were quickly discarded "to protect them from his clumsiness."

And despite his words, there is absolutely nothing clumsy about Jake. Not when it comes to sex. Not even with his cast. In fact, he's the best I've ever had. By far. A fact which both terrifies and pleases me. Because I'm still not sure if he's sticking around. And if he doesn't, am I now ruined for other men?

Sheila's words echo through my head. Relax. Enjoy the ride.

I trail my fingers along his ink patterns, focusing on them in an effort to help calm my mind.

Huh. Looks like the dragon's tail is partially covering up a surgical scar, the thin, raised line extending from his wrist to his lower arm. Working my way higher, I trace his collarbone, noticing for the first time that one side has a scar and the other has a bump.

The rhythmic rise and fall of his chest changes, and I glance up to find his eyes on mine.

I trace the bump again, comparing it to the flatness of the other side.

"I broke both of them," Jake says. "A couple years apart. This one has a plate and screws—" he indicates the flat side "—and they let the other one heal on its own."

"How about this one?" I point to his arm.

"Broke my wrist. Two plates, half a dozen screws each."

"All work-related?"

"Those? Yes. This one—" he touches the scar near his eye "—not so much."

"What happened?"

He hesitates, then hangs his head. "I had a fight with a Care Bear purse."

I stifle a laugh.

"In my defense, it was a change purse, and Tracy whacked me with it. One of those little metal ball thingies caught me." He gives me a stern look and holds up a finger. "But if anyone asks, I took a header into a handlebar."

"Got it." I nod, crossing my heart. "Which one was the worst?"

"For my pride? The purse. But if we're talking pain—the leg. Definitely." He grimaces. "Remember the triple jump?"

"Yeah."

"Remember how high they went?"

"Yeah. What, like thirty feet?"

He nods. "That's how high I was when I fell."

I wince. "Ouch."

"Yep."

"Does it still hurt?"

"Not really. Just more of a dull ache now. Mostly when I've been standing too long. Or if it's raining. How about you? You got any good scar stories?"

"No. Not like yours."

"But surely you've got something."

"Well…" I scrunch my nose, then raise an arm. "This right here—" I say, pointing to a faint raised scar along the side of my hand "—is from a calculator."

His chest bounces as he laughs. "Nerd scars. Totally hot." He kisses the top of my head. "I love it."

"Yeah, well, they say Mathletes have the highest rate of injury of any sport."

He shakes his head. "No. No one says that."

"Okay… Well, do they at least say that we should study some more? You know, to make sure we're doing our homework right?"

"Yes. *That* I believe they *do* say." He taps his lips with a finger. "In fact, now that I think about it, I *do* remember my surgeon saying something about doing exercises. To help my leg."

"And you're sure this is what he meant?"

"Yep."

"You sure your doctor's not a quack?"

"Nope. Totally respectable. Best in the business." He raises an eyebrow. "Any chance you want to try helping me heal a little faster?"

I purse my lips, pretending to contemplate his question while every cell in my body screams "yes." "Alright. But on one condition."

"What's that?"

"That I get a front row seat to some of those penis tricks I've heard so much about."

The wicked grin that stretches across Jake's face sends flickers of desire racing through every nerve.

"I thought you'd never ask."

CHAPTER TWENTY-TWO

Jake

It's weird. I'm lying here, Lauren sprawled across my chest, and instead of wondering which excuse I'm gonna use or how fast I can make my getaway, I'm wondering what I did to get this lucky. And if I can manage not to screw this up.

Because this is seriously uncharted territory for me. And I have no clue what to do. How to be there for someone else. How to work through things instead of picking up and leaving.

Shit.

I still haven't completely made up my mind about the whole comeback thing. What if I decide not to go back? What kind of impact will that have on us?

Holy crap. There's an us.

Lauren stirs, stretching her arms. A lazy smile works its way across her mouth. "Morning, handsome."

"Morning, gorgeous."

She sighs as I trail a finger down her back. "Did you sleep well?" I ask.

"Yep. Like a rock." She peeks up at me. "I love this place. I may never want to leave."

I chuckle. "I know, right?"

"How'd you find it?"

"Well, with all the travel, I've tested out a lot of places. I think Hurley and I ended up here once before a big event. We were kind of strapped for cash, and there was some other event going on that had all the usual places packed. This place was booked, too, but it turns out Bert's grandson rides, and he let us have a cancellation in exchange for a couple of autographs." I glance around the room. "It's clean, quiet, and comfy, and the diner has the best damn hot fudge brownie sundaes I've ever tasted."

"Wow. You should do commercials."

"And lose the anonymity? Nope."

"Well, I hate to shatter your illusions, but you are definitely good boyfriend material." A V forms between her eyebrows. "Unless that's your signature move." She shifts, uncertainty clouding her features. "Oh, crap. It is, isn't it?"

"Nope. Despite what you may think, last night was tailor-made for you. And me. I've wanted to do that ever since Kylie mentioned the forking incident. So thank you for indulging me."

Her expression relaxes, her cheeks pinkening. "My pleasure. And uh, just so you know, I may have been having similar thoughts."

"Ah. Great minds think alike."

Lauren grins. "Does that mean you're also wondering if Bert takes orders for breakfast deliveries?"

"I wasn't. But now I am. Have I told you how smart you are?"

"You may have mentioned it once or twice."

"Yeah, well, get used to it." I plant a kiss on her mouth, stopping any of her disagreements before she can make them.

I stare at a naked Lauren hovering in the doorway of the bathroom.

"You sure you don't want to join me?"

I huff a laugh and shift on the bed, trying to relieve some of the pressure in my groin. "Want? Yes. Physically able to? No." There is nothing sexy about having to drape my leg over the side of the tub. Especially when my hip spasms from the position. Plus, even though I know Bert keeps it clean, there's still something skeevy about taking a bath in a motel tub. "But this thing should be coming off soon." I tap my cast. "Raincheck?" Although where the hell am I gonna raincheck? Not like I can really commandeer Tracy and Craig's bathroom for some sexy bath time after I get my cast off. Maybe her place?

Or maybe it's time I start to think about looking for my own place.

The thought zooms through my head like a rider gunning through a straightaway.

I wait for the panic, but it doesn't come.

Huh. Weird.

"You okay over there?" Lauren asks.

"What? Yeah." Surprisingly. "Why?"

"You looked like you were deep in thought. Or like you smelled something rotten."

I shake my head, plastering a smile on my face. "Nope. I'm good. Go ahead and get your shower."

Lauren's forehead wrinkles.

"Uh-oh. That's *your* thinking face."

She nods. "I was just thinking that a good girlfriend would take care of her boyfriend. Especially if he's injured."

"Okay…"

"And you remember these hands?" She wiggles her fingers. "And how they're good for massages?"

"Yeah." She'd demonstrated her skill on several additional body parts last night. I'm a huge fan.

"Well, they're also really good for sponge baths."

The body part that enjoyed her "massages" the most last night tightens again.

"And, uh, if you're not doing anything tonight when we get back, I might have some free time in my schedule." She darts a look at the cramped bathroom. "I think it'll be a little more comfortable than here."

"Seriously. Are you in my head?" It's getting kind of freaky how we seem to be on the same wavelength. I kinda like it.

She grins. "No. But I'm guessing that's a yes?"

"Oh, that's a hell yes. But I'm only doing this so you don't feel like a bad girlfriend."

"I appreciate that. Thank you."

"My pleasure."

Lauren sighs and wraps her fingers around the steering wheel. "I don't want to leave."

"Well, we *could* stay here. But I'm pretty sure Bert's reached his delivery limit, and sooner or later, we're gonna need more food. Besides, we should get a move on, or we're gonna be late."

"Late for what?"

"For the final stop of the Lauren Gone Wild tour."

She presses her lips together, but a smile sneaks through anyway. "Just promise me there won't be any videos surfacing that I'll regret later."

"Damn. I *knew* I forgot something."

We ride in comfortable silence, every now and then singing along with the music, until we reach our destination.

Lauren stares out the windshield at the tattoo parlor. "Oh. Are you getting another tattoo?"

"Maybe. We'll see." I grab my crutches and extricate myself from the car, nodding her inside. "Come on."

Gunther's face creases into a smile, and he kicks his boots off the counter. "Jake! My favorite customer."

"He says that to all his customers," I say.

Gunther shrugs. "Maybe. Doesn't mean it's not true." He extends a hand to Lauren. "You must be Jake's friend. Let me know if this is what you were looking for. If not, no problem. I can make adjustments. Or we can do something else." He pulls a sheet of paper from under the counter and slides it toward Lauren.

Her eyes round into saucers, and they bounce back and forth between me and Gunther. "Wait. We're here for me?"

I nod, nervous anticipation churning in my gut when she turns her attention to the paper.

Wait. Why the hell am *I* nervous? I'm not the one getting my first tattoo. She can say no if she wants.

"Oh, wow," she breathes. "It's beautiful." She holds it out so I can see.

She's right. It is. In fact, it's perfect. The bottom is an open book, the pages gradually shifting into butterflies, which arc up like a rainbow.

Gunther traces the curve with a finger. "It's totally up to you, but from what Jake said, I'm guessing you're gonna want this someplace kinda hidden. It'll show with a swimsuit or with those cami things, but if we did it on your upper back, the butterflies could fly up and over your shoulder blade."

"Yes," she blurts out. "Do it." The thinking lines between her eyebrows furrow. "What exactly did Jake say?"

Gunther chuckles. "Dude waxed rather ineloquently for like thirty minutes. But I got the gist. That you were looking to open up. Make some changes. Spread your wings."

I shoot Gunther a dirty look. "Shut up, man. I did *not* wax ineloquently."

"Yeah. You did. Damn near talked my ear off."

"Lies," I say to Lauren. "All of them. Don't listen to him." Especially since it makes me sound like a teenage girl.

"Hmm…" Lauren studies me, the smirking smile playing at her lips. "Well that's a pity. Because I love it. And I think whoever designed it deserves a big thank you."

Pride swells in my chest. "Oh, well, in that case—"

"You're welcome," Gunther says.

Lauren chuckles and presses a kiss to the corner of my mouth. "Seriously. Thank you. It's perfect. I don't know how you're gonna top this."

Me neither. But I think I'm gonna have fun trying.

CHAPTER TWENTY-THREE

Lauren

Jake pauses inside the door of my condo and looks around. "Nice. It looks like you."

I follow his gaze around my living room. Nothing out of the ordinary, just a cozy, tidy space with comfortable yet serviceable furniture, books and photos scattered across various tables and lining my bookshelves, and a couple of paintings on the walls. "Thanks?"

He grins. "I like it."

"Yeah. Me, too." Even though it might not look like much, it feels good. Especially this time of day. The setting sun gives the room a soft glow. It always feels like a warm hug. "You want something to drink?"

"Maybe in a bit. We need to take care of that tattoo first."

"Oh. Right." It's been a couple of hours since we left Gunther's, and I plan to follow his post-tattoo instruction sheet to a T. Dumping my bag inside the door, I take Jake's backpack and set it next to mine. I pull out the supplies we picked up on the way home, lining up the soap, antiseptic ointment, and bandages on my kitchen counter. "My bathroom's definitely bigger than Bert's, but you'll probably have an easier time maneuvering out here."

"A grateful nation thanks you." Jake props himself against the counter. "Okay. Strip."

Even though we've had a significant amount of naked, sexy time over the past two days, his command still makes the butterflies in my stomach beat a nervous rhythm. It all still feels kind of surreal. Like it's almost too good to be true.

Calloused hands slide up my back, gently removing my shirt while leaving little explosions of pleasure in their wake. I shiver as he teases my bra strap off my shoulder.

"Cold?"

I shake my head.

"Ah. The *other* kinds of shivers. Got it." I can hear the smile in his voice, and the deep rumble near my ear does nothing to calm the hormones rushing excitedly to parts south. "Hold that thought. Let's take care of this first. Then we can take care of the *other* stuff."

"And by *other stuff*, you mean helping each other heal, right?"

"Yes. That's exactly what I mean." He whispers a kiss on my neck. "I'm so glad we're on the same page." Efficient fingers remove the bandages, and he gently cleans the area.

"How does it look?" I can't wait to see what it looks like when it's healed. Makes me kind of wish I was brave like Jake and would've put it somewhere visible. The fact that Gunther came up with that design based on what Jake told him amazes me. Both Gunther's artwork and Jake's insights.

"Looks great," he says, covering it again and moving my bra strap back in place. "If you wanna bring stuff to the shop, I can help you clean it and change the bandages."

I turn to face him. "Or, you could, you know…come over here."

"Or that." He wraps one arm around my waist, keeping the other on the counter for balance. "You know, I've actually been having some crazy thoughts."

"Oh? Crazy like whipped cream and hot fudge?"

His eyes darken, and a lascivious grin curves his lips. "Well, those too… But I was actually talking about crazy thoughts like maybe getting my own place."

"Oh. Wow."

"Yeah."

"Wait. Like, your own place for the next few months? Or longer?"

"Not a hundred percent sure yet, but I'm kinda thinking longer."

The thought of Jake around long-term sends little thrills of excitement through me. Concern soon follows. "Oh. Does that mean you're done with racing?"

Jake's Adam's apple bobs as he swallows. "Will you think less of me if I am?"

The vulnerability in his eyes squeezes my ribcage. "Of course not. It's a huge decision. A scary decision. And no one can make that decision but you."

The corner of his mouth quirks in the hint of a smile. "Thanks. You give really good pep talks."

"No problem. Go, Team, right?"

His smile widens. "Right. Go, Team." Shifting against the counter, he brushes a kiss against my collarbone. "While we're on the subject of team dynamics, yesterday you said something about me scaring the crap out of you." Another kiss. "What'd you mean by that?"

"Oh." I tilt my chin, giving him better access to my neck. "That." Pleasure hums through me. "I just meant that I thought you were intimidating."

"Oh, yeah?" He nibbles my earlobe.

"Uh-huh."

"Why?"

"Uh…" My brain cells try to process my thoughts. No easy feat with his continued ministrations to the sensitive skin behind my ear. "Because of how hot you are. And how confident. And how hot."

He chuckles. "I believe you said that one already."

"Oh. Right."

"And now?" he asks.

"Oh, my God. So hot." Burning, in fact. I may very well burst into flames right here in my kitchen. "But not so intimidating. Just a really good guy."

"For the record, you scared the crap out of me, too."

I pull back, giving him a questioning look. "I did?"

"Uh-huh. With your gigantic brain and your smart hobbies and your two jobs. Totally out of my league."

"What?" No one in the history of anyone has called me out of their league.

He crosses his heart. "Honest to God."

"And now?"

"Oh, you're still definitely out of my league, but I'm a hard worker." He winks. "I'll keep climbing the ranks."

Delight and desire curl through me. "Any chance you feel like putting in some more hard work tonight?"

"As a matter of fact, yes, I do."

"Great. Just follow the hall straight back. I'll get our stuff."

As Jake heads toward my bedroom, I grab the bags. My phone buzzes, and I pull it out. Crap. Five 9-1-1 texts from Megan.

Do I text her back?

Or do I ignore it?

Ignore it. After all, Hot Jake's in my bedroom waiting to get to work.

But what if this is the one time it really is an emergency?

It's never an emergency. And you deserve one more night of fun.

The merry-go-round of arguments slams to a halt when someone knocks on the door.

"Lauren?" Megan calls. "Are you in there? Are you okay?"

Oh, crap. What the hell is she doing here?

"Do I need to call 9-1-1?"

Crap, crap, crap. I tiptoe to my bedroom with the bags. "Stay here. I'll be right back." I wince. "Megan's here."

Jake nods. "Got it." I start to close the door but stop when he adds, "Uh, you may want to put on a shirt."

Oh. Right. I hustle back out front, wrestle my shirt in place, and put on my game face. The one that says I'm just here by myself. Alone. And definitely do not have a man waiting for me in the bedroom.

Oh, God. We're in trouble. My game face sucks.

Forcing my mouth into a smile, I open the door. "Hey. What's up?"

"What's up is that I just sent you five 9-1-1s."

"Sorry. I've been kind of busy."

"Yeah. With work, right?" Concern and suspicion war on her features.

"Yep. You know how spacy I get around end-of-quarter time."

"Uh-huh." Her eyes narrow. "Except it's not end of quarter, is it?"

"Uh…" Crap. I didn't think anyone paid attention to the weird calendar we operate on at school.

"Although it *does* seem like you've been busy." She pulls her phone out of her pocket and swipes at it a few times, then holds it out toward me. "With a certain someone?"

The pit in my stomach opens up as I stare at the screen. At the picture of me and Jake sitting at the Motocross event. Me, laughing at something he said.

Him, with his arm around me, a boyish grin on his face. We look happy. Like we belong together.

The gooey warmth flows through me again, but it's chased away by the stern expression on Megan's face.

"What. The. Hell?"

"Um… I was curious about Motocross. So he took me?" Yeah. That sounds plausible. Except for the fact that it came out like a question.

"Uh-huh. And were you also curious about what his tonsils tasted like?"

"Wha—?" The question dies on my lips as she flips to another picture. One of us mid-kiss.

Megan cocks an eyebrow. "Anything you want to tell me?"

"He's a really good kisser?"

She gives me a bland look. "I know."

"Oh. Right." My brain cells slowly come back online. "Wait. How'd you find these?"

"They popped up on a racing site."

"Why are you searching racing sites?" I didn't even know she liked racing.

"Two words—Luca Romano."

"Oh." Totally figures that I'd get busted because she's crushing on an Italian hottie Supercross star.

"If these pictures are correct, you lied. To my face. Right there." Megan jabs a finger at my sofa. "'Please tell me it's not Jake,' I said. 'It's not Jake,' you said."

"Okay. I lied. It's Jake."

"No shit. And seriously. What the hell? I thought you were smarter than that. Smarter than me." She shakes her head, disbelief slowly morphing into

174

curiosity. "Okay. I'm still pissed. But I'm also dying over here. Spill it. What's going on between you two?"

My eyes dart to the bedroom, and she gasps. "Is he here?"

My bedroom door squeaks open, and Jake appears in the doorway. "Yep."

Megan hisses and jabs a finger at Jake. "You!"

Jake crutches into the room and raises an eyebrow. "Whatever you've got to say, go ahead. I've got it coming."

She balls her hands at her sides, her lips pressed into a fine line. "You will *not* hurt my friend."

"He's not hurting me."

"Yet," Megan adds.

Jake locks eyes with me. "I promise I will never hurt Lauren." He holds my gaze for another beat before turning his attention to Megan. "And I owe you an apology. For how I acted when we...you know. I was a douche. And I'm sorry."

"Yeah, well..." She crosses her arms and glowers at him. "Temporary apology accepted. But so help me if you do that to her—"

"I won't."

"Okay." Megan gives a curt nod, her eyes bouncing back and forth between the two of us. "Holy crap. I still can't believe it."

Yeah. Join the club.

CHAPTER TWENTY-FOUR

Jake

Stretching out on my bed, I scroll through my phone, then punch dial. "Hey, Mom."

"Jake! What's wrong?"

"What? Nothing's wrong." I wince. She's practically wired to expect medical disasters when I call.

"Oh. Phew. Well, then, to what do I owe the pleasure?"

"Can't a son just call his mother to say hi?"

"Depends. Are you the son?"

"Uh, yeah."

"Then no. You're not exactly the chatty phone guy. So, what's up? How's your leg?"

"Okay. I've got another couple of weeks with this cast, then I should get a walking boot. Still a ways to go."

"But at least it's headed the right direction. That's good."

"Yeah, it is." I take a deep breath, releasing it slowly. "Hey, Mom? Can I talk to you about something?"

"Of course. As long as you and your sister aren't picking on each other again."

"No, Mom. It's not about me and Tracy." I blow out another calming breath. "What would you say if I decided not to race anymore?"

"I'd say hallelujah."

"Seriously?"

"Well, yeah. You go sixty miles an hour and rocket thirty feet in the air. I love you, but you're kinda crazy."

"Says the woman who currently works at a nudist colony."

"Hey. At least no one here is in danger of landing in the hospital. Except for Barry. But that was because he threw his back out having sex."

"Ew. Mom!"

"Relax. It wasn't with me. Poor Marge," she murmurs. "Anyway. What were we talking about?"

"Definitely not you and your kinky clients."

"They're not kinky. They're just regular people who don't like to be inhibited by convention. And who happen to tip very well. But back to you. Are you seriously thinking about giving up racing?"

"Yeah. I am." I swallow down another wave of unease. "Would you think I was a quitter?"

She snorts. "No. Definitely not. I might wonder if Tracy's been slipping something into your food, but I wouldn't think of you as a quitter." Her tone softens. "Why would you think that?"

Doubt squeezes my windpipe. "Because it's the only thing I've been good at. And I'd be giving it up."

"Oh, Jake. Stop that. You know that's not true. You're good at plenty of things. And you always knew the racing thing wasn't forever. Right?"

"Yeah. I guess."

"Then what's the real issue?"

Shit. Leave it to Mom to keep right on jackhammering.

"Because of how hard you always fought. For me. And you. And us." I gulp. "You never quit."

"Yeah, well, I didn't really have a choice. Single mom, two kids… I just had to keep moving forward. There was no room for quitting. But what you're going through is totally different."

"Still feels like quitting, though."

"Maybe. Or maybe it's just the universe opening up another door for you."

"Who are you and what have you done with my mother?"

"Hey. I can be philosophical."

"Since when? Oh, my God. It's the nudies. They got to you, didn't they?"

She stifles a laugh. "Jake, stop. I'm just saying that sometimes things might not be as bad as they initially seem. Take raising you and your sister, for instance. There were days I thought you'd both drive me crazy. Now you've both grown into wonderful adults, and I couldn't be prouder."

The emotions thicken my throat again.

"And as an adult," she continues, "you don't need my permission. You can do whatever you want.

You just need to follow your heart. What's your heart telling you, Jake?"

"You mean besides the fact that I have a seriously cool Mom?"

"Of course. That's a given."

I bite back a smile as I take stock of the jumble of feelings I'm not used to dealing with.

Because if I'm not mistaken, my heart's telling me that I might be ready for my life to move in a different direction. That I've got a really good thing going here, and that I don't want to mess it up.

And that my greatest fear is that I will.

I tap a beat against my empty breakfast plate. "So, uh, you got a few minutes?"

Tracy glances at her watch. "Sure. What's up?"

"I talked to Mom last night."

"Uh-oh. She didn't talk you into visiting her at the nudie colony, did she?"

"No. Although apparently there's a friends and family discount. Clothing optional." We both shudder. "I called her to discuss some things." My gut clenches as I prepare for my next words. "I'm done racing."

Her eyes light up. "Really?"

"You don't have to look so happy about it."

"Oh. Sorry. It's just—"

"I know, I know, hurtling through the air on a death missile." She grins as I air quote one of Mom's favorite ways to describe my job.

"Well, that," she says. "Plus the fact that maybe you'd consider sticking around?"

"Funny you should mention that…"

"What? Seriously?"

"Yep. I've kind of been thinking it might not be the worst thing in the world to put some roots down. At least on a trial basis."

"Wow. That must've been some talk with Mom."

"Nah. I was thinking about that before last night. I've been thinking about it for a little while now, actually." With a significant increase over the weekend. "And, uh, you should probably also know that I'm dating someone." Might as well keep the revelations coming. Especially since Lauren and I plan on spending a lot more time together.

"What?" Tracy's coffee sloshes over the side of her cup as it hits the table. "Who?"

"Lauren."

"Your boss, Lauren?"

"Yep."

"Wow. I don't know what to say. On so many levels." She shakes her head. "I mean, one—she's your boss. And two—you're actually dating someone. Which implies a relationship. Which I didn't think you were capable of."

"Gee. Thanks."

"Oh, come on. Not like I'm telling you something you haven't said yourself a million times."

As much as it ever pains me to admit that my sister's right, in this case, she is. I *have* said it. On numerous occasions. "Yeah, well, she's different."

Tracy's eyes become saucer-round, and she gasps. "Is she *The One*? Oh, my God. Is she the reason you're staying?"

I shift in my seat. "What? No. We just started officially dating this weekend."

"Eh. You might be surprised. Sometimes love doesn't take all that long."

"What? Who said anything about love?" I know I definitely haven't. And neither has Lauren. This is just…something after the friendship stage.

"Uh, your face." She wags her finger toward me. "That dopey look in your eyes."

I bat her finger away. "Shut up. I do not have a dopey look."

She snorts. "Yeah, you do. All the time, in fact. But this one's different." I scowl, but she just grins. "Come on. It's sweet. And exciting. Do you know how long I've been waiting for you to settle down and get married?"

"Whoa! I hope you listen to your patients better than you listen to me. Because I did *not* say anything about marriage."

"Part of being a good psychologist is listening between the lines."

"That's not a thing." Is it?

"And you can fight it all you want, but sooner or later…" She starts twitching her shoulders, then launches into the chorus of Gloria Estefan's *Rhythm Is Gonna Get You*, singing 'marriage' instead of 'rhythm.'

"Oh, my God. I hate you so much."

"Love you, too." She grins.

Ugh. I seriously need to get my own place.

And possibly a new sister.

I scroll down the page, stopping every now and then to check out potential apartments. Rent around here is more expensive than I'd anticipated, but if I go out of the city a little more, I think it'll be doable.

Might not be a bad idea to have Lauren take a look at my finances, though. Make sure I'm not missing anything. After all, what good is having a Mathlete for a girlfriend if you can't ask for her help once in a while?

I shake my head in wonder. I'm not sure which part is more surprising—the girlfriend part or the Mathlete part.

My phone vibrates on the desk next to me. Hurley's name flashes on the screen, and I answer. "Hey, man. What's up?"

"Dude. Don't hate me, but I may have slipped a little about your whole maybe not coming back thing."

"Nah. It's fine. And actually, it's not a maybe anymore."

"Ah, man. You mean you're done?"

"Yep." As much as saying the words still stings, I have to admit that it feels lighter to not have the comeback question lingering. To feel like I can finally focus on something else and move on. Even if I still don't quite know what I'm moving on *to*.

"Dude. That sucks."

"Yeah. I know. I'm gonna miss you guys." My chest squeezes at the thought of not hanging out with them anymore on a regular basis. Shit. That might be the toughest part about retiring—missing the camaraderie.

"Well… Maybe you don't have to…"

CHAPTER TWENTY-FIVE

Lauren

I cringe when I see Kylie's name on my phone. I seriously need to tell her.

Jake's been spending a lot more time at my place, and while we've been lucky so far, we definitely don't need a repeat of the whole Megan incident. Although, all things considered, Megan's taken the whole me and Jake thing remarkably well. I mean, nobody died, so that's a plus. Of course, that could be because Jake told her he'd get her a ticket to the next Supercross event so she can get up close and personal with Luca, and she's just waiting to kill Jake until after that.

Steeling myself, I swipe across the screen. "Hey, Kylie. What's up?"

"Oh, good. I'm glad you picked up. Is there any chance you can open the shop today? I just got summoned to City Hall, I can't get a hold of Jake, and Aunt Sheila's taking Uncle Pete to a doctor's appointment."

"Oh. Is that good or bad? I mean, the City Hall thing, not Uncle Pete's appointment."

"Not sure yet. I'm hoping good, but I'll let you know. So… Can you do it? Please?"

"Yeah. Sure. I'm not working at the college today, and I was planning to go into the shop a little later anyway."

"Thanks. You're a lifesaver." She hangs up before I can say anything else.

Hmm… If I'm lucky, we'll get good news about the program, and I can subtly slide my news in while she's high on victory. Maybe this won't be so bad after all.

I'm putting the finishing touches on the latest updates to the website, noting our new one-on-one sessions, when Kylie bursts through the front door.

Uh-oh. From the grim set of her mouth and the laser death eyes, I'm guessing she got some bad news about the program.

She scans the shop. "Anyone else here?"

I shake my head. "Kylie. I'm so sorry."

She barks out a laugh. "Yeah. I'll bet."

"We'll figure something out." Maybe. If we're lucky. "I mean, I have a little money socked away in my 401K, and maybe the bank will refinance—"

"What the hell are you talking about?"

"The shop. Since we didn't get the bid—"

"Oh, we got the bid, alright."

"Oh. That's great." But then why in the hell is she so pissed?

Kylie narrows her eyes. "We got it with Spence."

"What?"

"We tied. We're co-winners."

"Oh. Wow. That's...unexpected." And explains a lot.

Kylie snorts. "Yeah. You know what else was unexpected? Spence sidling up to me after they made the announcement and talking to me about his friend Hurley. And his friend Hurley meeting my sister. And her boyfriend. At an event last weekend. When you were 'working.'" She air quotes the last word.

My gut takes a nosedive toward my shoes. "Kylie, I can explain—"

"Save it." She holds up a hand and paces the floor. "I mean, it's bad enough that you two are sneaking around behind my back, but the fact that I have to learn about it from *him*?"

"Sorry I'm late, I was..." Jake pauses just inside the door, his eyes darting back and forth between me and Kylie. "Am I interrupting something?"

I give my head a terse shake, telepathically trying to tell him to get out of here while he still can. It doesn't work.

Kylie spins to face him. "Yes! Apparently, you're interrupting my sister's brain waves."

"What?" Jake's forehead crinkles in confusion.

"That's the only explanation I can think of for why she'd think this is a good idea." She wags her finger back and forth between me and Jake. "Especially after we both decided the whole workplace romance thing was a *bad* idea." She glares at me with her laser beam eyes.

"*You* decided. I just didn't argue with you."

"Do you know what kind of risk you've exposed us to?" Kylie asks.

"What? Are you kidding me right now? You did the exact same thing!"

"Yeah. And clearly I was an idiot." She pinches the bridge of her nose. "Look. I just thought you'd be smarter than me."

"Oh, my God. You sound like Megan. Why can't people accept that I am a grown woman who can make her own choices? Seriously! I mean, I do everything for everyone else. I gave up my promotion for you. For this." I wave my hand around the shop. "You asked for my help, and I came running. Megan asks for help, and I come running. So I decide to do something for myself for a change. So what? I deserve to have a little fun every now and then."

"Is that what this is? Just a little fun?" Kylie asks.

"Maybe. I don't know." I dart a glance at Jake, but he looks like he's still trying to figure out what the hell's going on.

Kylie shrugs. "Well, don't come crying to me when it blows up in your face."

"Wow. Way to be supportive."

"Oh. You mean like you were supportive of me and AJ?"

"That was different. AJ's a tool. He was clearly just using you."

"Yeah, well, maybe *Jake's* using *you*."

"What? You're crazy. If you'll recall," I say to her, "*you're* the one who kept saying we weren't taking full advantage of him. In fact, *you're* the one who wanted to hire him in the first place. So if anything, *we're* using *him*. On second thought, maybe I am using him. Maybe I'm using him to add some excitement to my life. Would that really be such a bad thing?"

"Is that true?" Jake's voice is flat. Dangerously calm. "Are you really just using me?"

Shit. In the heat of the moment, I'd completely forgotten about him.

He clenches and unclenches the handles of his crutches, and his jaw ticks as he watches us.

"What? No. That's not what I meant." I replay my words. "Okay. Maybe that is what I meant. But I thought you were okay with it."

He nods, his Adam's apple bobbing. "Yeah. Sure. I did say that."

"Great!" Kylie says, sarcasm in her tone. "We're all using each other. One big dysfunctional work family. This'll go well," she mutters.

"Yeah... About that." Jake shifts on his crutches. "I just got a job offer. With the tour. So maybe don't go counting on me as part of the family."

His words punch me in the gut. "Oh. Uh...That's great."

His eyes search mine. "Really?"

No. Not really. It's awful. Especially if it means he's leaving. But I can't ask him to stay. Not if he wants to go. That wouldn't be fair. "Yeah. Sure. You should do what makes you happy. This whole thing between us was moving too fast anyway."

"Yeah. Okay. Glad we're on the same page." His jaw ticks. "I, uh, think I need to get a little air."

"Yeah. Me, too," Kylie says as Jake disappears out the front door. "I'll be in the back. Trying to figure out what the hell just happened."

Yeah. That makes two of us.

CHAPTER TWENTY-SIX

Jake

I guess there's a reason why workplace romances aren't a good idea.

Because when they go bad, it's awkward as fuck.

Thank God Lauren's been keeping her distance. She's only been in a handful of times since the blowup last week, and even then, she's stayed up front. At least without her in the shop, it's only slightly awkward as fuck.

I am definitely on Kylie's shit list, although less so since I agreed to stay on for a few more weeks. Give them some time to figure out what to do until Pete's back regularly.

After all, I'm not a total douche.

Not about that, anyway.

God, I should've seen it coming. Should've known Lauren was just in it for the thrill. After all, she's right. We *did* have that conversation. I actually told her I'd be happy to help her expand her horizons. I just didn't think she really meant it.

Not like that.

Dumbass.

That's why you do one-nighters. No attachments, no commitments, no feeling like you're the biggest idiot ever.

I check the chain stretch of the bike on the stand, pushing away the memory of our lesson. Her soft curves, her vanilla scent.

My groin tightens.

Dammit! Why does the thought of her still make me so crazy?

Maybe it's like when I was cooped up after my surgeries. Maybe I just need to get out. Get her out of my system. Hook up with someone else. Someone on my level. Someone who's into the same thing I am—meaningless sex. Yeah. That totally makes sense. It's just like wiping out during a race. You've just gotta pick yourself up and get back out there. And there's no better time like the present.

I glance at my clothes. Under normal circumstances, I'd go home and change. Put a little effort into how I look. But these aren't normal circumstances. This is just a means to an end. A cleansing of the palate. Plus, my cargo shorts and T-shirt are about the only things that make sense. My jeans don't fit over my cast.

And it's not like I think I'll have any trouble finding a willing participant. Especially if I play the professional athlete card.

Ex-athlete card.

My gut clenches.

Shit. Am I making the right choice?

I thought I was. Last week I would've said hanging it up and moving on was definitely the right thing to do. No question. But things seem a little murkier now. I'm not quite so sure what I want.

Except to get out of my head for a while.

'Cause this overthinking thing really *is* a bitch.

I pay the driver and work my way out of the car.

"You gonna need a ride on the flip side?" he asks.

"Not if I'm lucky."

Of course, I'll have to do a little vetting. Make sure whoever I end up with has her own place. Preferably one without too many stairs.

Damn. Seriously. Stop overthinking this.

Right. Okay. Here we go. Go, Team.

I bite back a curse. Yeah. I seriously need to get Lauren out of my head.

I hobble through the front door and scan the bar. It's busy. Noisy, but with a relaxed feel. Low lighting to either add to the ambience or to help make the meaningless hookups that much easier. Feels like any number of pickup bars I've frequented over the years.

Settling at an empty spot at the bar, I order a beer, then scan the room.

Yeah, I've missed this. The thrill of the hunt. The familiar surge of anticipation.

Where is that familiar surge of anticipation?

Damn. I really *have* been off my game for way too long. Good thing I'm here tonight. Get back to where I should be.

But where is that exactly?

Should I be on tour, even if I'm not competing? Or should I be here, with family?

Guilt gnaws at my gut.

I haven't told Tracy yet. About what happened with Lauren or about the job offer. And Reece... I don't even want to see the look on his face when I tell him. He was so happy when I said I'd be sticking around.

Shit. Enough of that. No chick's gonna wanna take you home if you're all mopey.

Okay. *Some* chicks will. But those chicks have issues. And I'm strictly issue-free tonight.

Right. Showtime.

Years of experience allow me to quickly sort through my options. The redhead in the corner is giving me the eye, but she's got too many friends with her. The platinum-blonde across the room could work, although she's already clinging to that guy like she might not let go. And I definitely don't want a clinger. Neither does he, from the panicked look in his eye.

"Almost makes you feel sorry for him, doesn't it?" A brunette slides into the seat next to me and nods toward the couple. "Haven't seen you in here before. You new to the area? Or just passing through?"

"Not sure yet."

She arches an eyebrow.

"Kind of in recuperation mode right now." I swivel a bit, revealing my cast.

"Ah." She sips her drink, ruby lips curling around her straw as her eyes stay locked on me.

Oh, yeah. We've got a live one.

"So," she says, nodding to my leg, "do I get to hear the story? I'm Beth, by the way."

"Hi, Beth. I'm Jake. Let me freshen up that drink for you."

"For real?" Well-manicured nails give my arm a light squeeze. "Motocross? Like, on the tour and everything?"

"Yep." At least for now. I haven't officially said anything about retirement. Besides, she seems pretty excited. Wouldn't want to do anything to jeopardize my chances of sealing the deal.

"Can I get your autograph? And maybe a picture?"

Crap. She's not gonna be one of those women who keep mementos of her conquests, is she?

Does it really matter?

A familiar voice tells me it does, but I push it away. I don't want to hear her voice anymore. Definitely not tonight. And definitely not right now.

I nod. "Sure. Why not?"

"Oh, great. My cousin's kid is huge into Motocross. He's gonna freak." I must look as relieved as I feel, because she wrinkles her nose. "You didn't think I was one of those weirdo fame-bangers, did you?"

I run a hand across the back of my neck. "Actually…"

She grimaces. "I promise. This is legit." She pulls out her phone and scrolls through several pictures before holding it out to me. A boy twice the size of Reece is suited up in typical Motocross gear standing next to a bike. He's covered head to toe in dirt and looks like he enjoyed every minute of how it got there. "This is Marcus. He's nine and probably going to give his mother a heart attack before he's ten. Total daredevil."

I grin. "I can relate."

She hands her phone to the bartender, who snaps a couple of pictures of us mugging for the camera. "You got any tips I can take back to her?" she asks when we're done.

"Invest in good insurance."

"For her or him?"

"Both."

Her lips twitch. "You're funny."

"I try."

Huh. This might be easier than I think. She's nice. And attractive. But maybe it would be easier if she wasn't so nice. If she *was* actually in it for the fame-bang.

After all, this is supposed to be string-free.

Beth licks her lips. "You wouldn't by any chance want to get out of here, would you?"

I open my mouth to say yes, more than a little shocked to hear myself say "No" instead.

Her eyebrows dart to her hairline. "Oh, uh…"

"Shit. What I meant to say was I'd love to, but, uh, I don't think I can."

What? Why the hell not? What the hell is wrong with you? This is exactly why you came out tonight.

"My leg's not feeling so great. I think I'm gonna head home." I give Beth a weak smile as I slide off my stool and get my crutches in place. "Sorry. Say hi to Marcus for me."

"Yeah. Okay." Bewilderment clouds her features.

I kick myself all the way out the door.

What the hell, man? You had a perfectly good opportunity. An opportunity you would've jumped at just a couple of months ago.

A thought bolts through my head leaving a trail of discomfort and confusion in its wake.

Maybe I turned Beth down tonight because I don't actually want to be that same guy from a couple months ago.

But if I don't wanna be *that* guy, who *do* I want to be?

CHAPTER TWENTY-SEVEN

Lauren

Thank God I have so much work to do. Nothing quite like throwing yourself into Excel spreadsheets to take the sting out of epic failure.

Epic *personal* failure.

I'm still trying to avoid the epic *financial* failure part of the equation. Hopefully that will be easier now that we won the City Bike Program. Or kind of won. At least theoretically.

And at least Kylie's still so busy being pissed off at Spence and the whole co-winner thing that she really hasn't had time to harp on me about Jake. Which is great, because I'm doing enough of that on my own. I mean, what good is being smart if you're just gonna go out and lose your head around the first hot guy who makes you feel special? How dumb is that?

I rub my eyes, trying to corral my thoughts. Come on. How are we gonna make ends meet?

Think, Lauren. Think. And not about how much I miss Jake.

Because despite the hurt, I do miss him.

I miss his laugh and his easy-going manner and how comfortable he makes me feel.

Made me feel.

Argh! Focus!

And not on that gooey sensation I get when I think about him in bed with hot fudge sauce…

I'll probably never be able to eat another brownie sundae ever again.

Dammit!

Effectively pissed at the thought that he's ruined my favorite dessert, I throw myself back into the task at hand.

Or try to, anyway. There are just so many freaking variables.

Who's gonna do which parts of the bike program? Will we split the money fifty-fifty, or is it gonna be some kind of ratio? If it's a ratio, will it be stable or will it vary month to month?

And what about when Jake leaves? I know he's staying around here for another couple of weeks, but will Uncle Pete be at full strength by then? Are we gonna have to hire someone else? Or can Kylie and I manage to limp along for a while?

And exactly how many more months can we manage to limp along financially? What the heck's gonna happen when that balloon payment comes due? Will the bank refinance us if we can't scrape it together? And what are we gonna do if we can't?

The weight of expectations sits heavy on my shoulders. And my neck.

An hour later, I have a full-blown headache and no more idea of what to do or where we stand than when I sat down at my kitchen table.

After popping a couple ibuprofen and chugging some water, I sit back down. If I'm not making any headway with finances right now, at least I can be productive in other ways. Or try to, anyway.

I click to the shop's website, intent on updating the schedule of events, but find myself typing Jake's name into the search engine instead. After all, customers will have questions, right? They'll probably want to know why he left. What he's doing. He really didn't tell us anything about his job offer. Maybe there's something online.

Right. The fact that you miss his panty-dropping smile and gorgeous eyes has nothing to do with it.

Finding nothing on the typical trade sites, I log into social media, ignoring the voices inside my head. Because, yeah, I know this is pathetic and an epically bad idea, but what the hell else am I supposed to do? Desperate times call for desperate measures, right?

Oh, crap. When the hell did I delve into desperate territory? I've *never* been in desperate territory before.

This is bad.

My eyes widen, and my gut drops.

Shit. This is *really* bad.

Because there, on the screen, is a picture of Jake cozying up to a gorgeous brunette. The tag shows it's from a local pick-up bar I know Megan likes to frequent, and if the timestamp is correct, it's from just a few days ago.

My gut drops. He's moved on already?

I am such a stupid idiot. A naïve, stupid idiot.

Of course he's moved on already. Because obviously you didn't mean as much to him as he did to you.

Oh, my God, I feel sick.

I need some fresh air. And a change of scenery. And somewhere I can't connect to the internet and continue to torture myself.

Okay. So three out of four.

The arboretum is an internet connection-less change of scenery with nothing *but* fresh air. Unfortunately, it's full of torture.

Because *of course* my mind rubberbands back to that night on the bench over there. Curled up against him. Feeling safe. Secure.

Feeling right.

I rub my chest. Great. Now I feel sick *and* like someone's stabbed me in the chest.

Come on, Lauren! Get a grip! You didn't even know him that long! You dated Derek for an entire year of college and didn't even feel this crappy when he broke up with you. And that was the year Dr. Martin was adjusting your birth control pills and you were a hormonal mess!

Huh. Maybe that's the problem. Maybe my hormones are all out of whack and *that's* what's causing my freak-out. Yeah. Maybe it's some kind of weird early menopause thing. Not that I really look forward to hot flashes, but at least then I don't have to give up my favorite dessert. Or find a new relaxation spot.

Because if not, the arboretum might be off-limits for me, too.

Crap.

I pull up in front of Aunt Sheila's house armed with a couple bottles of wine. I'm not sure who needs it more at this point—me or her.

"Hey," I say, when she holds the door open for me. "Thanks for letting me come over."

"Phfft. You know you're welcome anytime. Especially when you bring presents." She takes the bottles and envelops me in a hug. Her eyebrows draw together as she pulls back and studies me. "What's going on? You sounded kind of odd on the phone. And don't take this the wrong way, but you're not looking so good, either. Are you sick?"

"Huh? No. I'm fine." Physically, anyway. Mentally and emotionally, however…

I rub my chest again, forcing a swallow past the tangle of emotions lodged in my throat. Come on, Lauren. Keep it together. "How are you guys?"

"We're fine." Aunt Sheila gives me another once-over, then lets go and opens the wine. "Especially now that Pete's doing therapy. Gets him out of the house and out of my hair. I don't know who'll be happier for him to get back to the shop—me or him."

I try to crack a smile, but it must be as weak as it feels, because Aunt Sheila gets that intense look again. "Alright. Out with it. What's going on?" she asks.

"Nothing. I'm fine." Inhaling, I let out a controlled exhale, trying to keep my emotions in check.

"Bullshit." Aunt Sheila purses her lips, her eyes narrowed. "I know you. And I know how much you like to keep things bottled up inside. And I also know about what's going on with the shop right now and with Jake taking a new job. So, unless I'm mistaken, and we both know that doesn't happen all that often—" she says with a wink "—you've got some serious unloading to do."

I tamp down the surge of emotions once again, but it's no use. The pressure builds behind my eyes, and before I know it, the tears are leaking out as quickly as my words. "I just feel so overwhelmed right now. There's the shop, with its finances and not knowing how this is all gonna work out, and I don't wanna let anyone down by not being able to figure this out, and Jake's already moved on, and I can't eat brownie sundaes or go to the arboretum anymore, and I think I may be in menopause."

Aunt Sheila presses her lips together, her expression a mixture of empathy and amusement. "Oh, honey. How long has all that been stewing in there?" She circles my head with a finger.

I shrug.

She gives me another long look, then nods. "How about you take a couple of breaths, take a few sips of wine, and then we'll sift through this piece by piece."

Half an hour later, my chest doesn't feel quite so tight, and my brain doesn't feel quite so clogged. I huff a laugh. "And here I thought I was doing such a good job of holding things together."

Aunt Sheila gives me a hard look. "Holding things together and holding things in are two very different concepts."

I sigh. "I know."

"No one can read your mind, you know."

I heave another sigh. "I know."

"And I seriously doubt you're going through menopause."

I grimace. "Yeah. I know."

"So…" Aunt Sheila swirls the remaining wine around her glass. "Now that I've gotten through that skull of yours that *no one* knows what the future holds and that *we are all in this together*—" she gives me a pointed look "—let's tackle the Jake issue."

"Must we?"

She raises an eyebrow.

"Ugh. Fine." I fortify myself with a swallow of wine. "In a nutshell? He's hot, I'm an idiot, he's moved on, and I can't ever eat brownie sundaes again. Oh. And I have a tattoo."

"What?"

"Yep." I stand up and turn around, lifting up the back of my shirt.

"Oh. Wow. That's—"

"Asinine? Un-Lauren-like? Proof that I'm a moron?"

"I was going to say beautiful."

"Oh. Yeah. That, too." I pull my shirt down and collapse back into my seat. "I got it that weekend you guys helped at the shop." The best weekend of my sad, pathetic life.

"What happened between you two?"

"I don't know. One minute I'm yelling at Kylie, the next, he's talking about leaving because he got a job offer." I run my finger around the bottom of my wine glass. "And there may have been a bit in between there where Kylie accused him of using us and I said we were using him."

"Ouch."

"Yeah."

"Did you try to talk to him about it?"

"No. Because that's when he told us he was leaving. And then he walked out. And I didn't follow him."

"Don't you think you *should* talk to him about it?"

"Maybe. But what good would it do? He's already moved on." I fill her in on what I found online. "Plus, it's not fair to him. If he wants to go, he should go. I know how hard it was for him to give up racing. If he has the chance to still be part of that world, he should."

"Well, that's very magnanimous of you."

"Thanks."

"Stupid, but magnanimous." She shakes her head. "You know what? It's not even magnanimous. It's just stupid. And a cop out."

"What? You did just hear the part about him moving on, right?"

"Maybe the picture means he moved on. Maybe it's just a picture of him with a fan. Who knows? What I *do* know is that I love your tattoo."

"Uh, thanks?" Not quite where I thought this was going...

"And I hope you keep doing that."

"What? Getting more tattoos?"

"No. Getting out of your comfort zone. Spreading your wings. Learning to fly." She gives me another long look. "You know what else I see in that tattoo?"

I shake my head.

"Someone who's fighting to be free. Fighting for what she wants."

The fist around my throat tightens.

I agree with her. That's what I see, too.

The question is, what do I really want?

CHAPTER TWENTY-EIGHT

Jake

Reece wanders into the living room and climbs onto the sofa next to me, settling against my hip. "Whatcha doin'?"

"Making a list."

"For Santa?"

"No. Not that kind of list."

"Oh. Are you gonna be around when Santa comes this year?"

"I'm not sure I'll be here then."

"Why not?"

"Because I might have a new job, and I might have to travel."

"But why? I thought you were gonna stay here. Don't you like it here? I like having *you* here." He cocks his head and studies me with wide, earnest eyes.

As expected, the knife twists in my chest.

Shit.

I rub my sternum, trying to ease the ache.

"Uncle Jake, are you okay?" His forehead furrows. "Does your chest hurt?"

"Yeah, buddy. But it's fine." Or it will be, once I man up and tell them I'm leaving.

Reece hops off the couch and scurries out of the room. "Mo-om! Uncle Jake's having chest pains!"

Crap. "Reece! It's not—"

"Not what?" Tracy enters the room and crosses it in quick strides, Reece on her heels. Concern etches her features. "What kind of chest pains? Are you short of breath? Do I need to call an ambulance?"

"What? No. It's not that kind of chest pain."

"Are you sure? How about leg pain? Swelling?"

I roll my eyes. "It's not a DVT or a pulmonary embolism."

"What's a pullomary emmalism?" Reece asks.

"A very serious issue that the doctor told us to be aware of," Tracy replies.

"I swear to you, this is not a blood clot." I hold my hand up in oath. "It's more like that pain you get when you have to tell someone something but you really don't wanna tell 'em."

Tracy continues to give me the stink eye as she sinks down onto the other side of the sofa and pulls Reece into her lap. "Hmm… Would we happen to be the people you don't wanna tell?"

"Yep." I take a deep breath, steeling myself. "So, I kinda got a job offer."

"Oh! That's great!" The excitement in Tracy's eyes gradually dims. "Ah. But it's not around here, is it?"

"Bingo. It's with the tour. So, I'd still be able to stop by every now and then, but…"

"Not here permanently. Got it."

"You're leaving? But I thought you were gonna stay here and play dinosaurs and cars with me. You said so." Reece's lower lip trembles, and the ache returns.

"I know. And I'm sorry, buddy."

Tracy ruffles Reece's hair. "Uncle Jake has to do what's right for Uncle Jake." She gives me a hard look. "You *are* doing what's right for you, right?"

"Yes." I stare at my list. "No. I don't know." I flop my head against the back of the couch.

"What's this?" She holds out her hand, and I give her the yellow legal pad.

"A pro and con list."

Her eyebrows jump. "Since when do you make pro and con lists?"

"Since I have no clue who I am or what I want to do or who I want to be when I grow up."

"I wanna be a dinosaur when I grow up," Reece says.

Tracy squeezes him. "We know. Hey. Why don't you go play in your room? I think Uncle Jake and I need to have a chat."

"Okay." He pops off her lap, pausing and looking at me. "Promise you won't leave while I'm in my room."

"I promise." I wait until Reece leaves, then blow out a breath. "Shit. That kid…"

"Yeah. I know. If I wanted to play dirty, I could probably just sic him on you. Have him wear you down."

"Thanks for not playing dirty."

"*Yet.* I reserve the right to pull him out later if I need to." She peruses the pro and con list again. "You suck at these, by the way."

"Gee. Thanks."

She holds it up. "I can't tell if the pro side is pro leaving or pro going. Same with the con side."

I lean over and tap the paper. "The pro side is pro taking the job, and the con side is me staying."

"So, we're a con?"

"What? No. That's not…" I hiss an exhale and rake my fingers through my hair. "Shit."

"And why is Lauren on both sides?"

"What?" I lean over and look at the paper again. Son of a bitch. She *is* on both sides. Several times. "I don't know. I just…" I let my head flop back against the couch again. "This sucks."

"What sucks?"

"This. This whole planning and futuring and trying to figure out who the hell I really am."

"You mean adulting?"

"Yeah."

"Join the club."

"Is it too late to get a refund on my membership?"

"Yep." She grins. "So why, exactly, is Lauren on both sides?"

"Uh… Because we kind of broke up."

"Why? What'd you do?"

"What do you mean? I didn't do anything."

"Are you sure?"

"Yeah." I gnaw my lip. "Pretty sure. Okay, maybe like ninety percent sure."

Tracy rolls her eyes. "Alright. Walk me through it."

I walk her through the events at the shop.

"And you just left?" she asks.

"Yeah."

"Have you tried to talk to her?"

"No."

"Why the hell not?"

"Because she said things were moving too fast."

"Yeah. *After* you told her you were taking another job."

"So?"

"So... She was probably surprised. And hurt. Kinda like how Reece and I are feeling right now."

"Yeah. Sorry about that. You know I appreciate everything you guys have done for me."

"I know. But we're not talking about us right now. Back to you and Lauren."

"I told you. There *is* no me and Lauren."

"Whatever." She waves my protest away like a bad smell. "How did it feel when she said she was using you?"

"Like crap. Like she ripped my heart out." I rub my chest, the ache blossoming once again. "I thought she was different, you know?"

"Different, how?"

"That she really liked me for me." I shove my fingers through my hair. "I think she really messed me up. I went to a bar the other night and turned down a perfectly good woman. That *never* happens."

"Oh, shit."

"Yeah, I know. I think Lauren broke me."

Tracy clamps her lips together. I can't quite tell if she's trying not to laugh or trying to keep her thoughts to herself.

"What?"

She shakes her head.

"Come on. Let me have it."

"I'm not sure you want it."

I roll my eyes. "What good's having a smart-ass therapist sister if she's not gonna give me her professional opinion on what a pathetic loser I am?"

She studies me, her lips twisted to the side like she always does when she's weighing her words. "Promise you won't freak out?"

"Uh-oh. That bad, huh?"

"Depends on how you look at it."

"Just say it. I'm a gigantic loser who's almost thirty, living with his sister, and can't even pick up women anymore."

Tracy cocks an eyebrow. "More like a great guy who's a gigantic idiot because he hasn't figured out that he's in love."

"What?"

"Sorry to have to be the one to break it to you, but…" She shrugs.

Her words continue to hammer at me, and my chest feels like it's caving in on itself. I double over, trying to catch my breath. "I take it back. Maybe I am having a pulmonary embolism."

The cushion next to me depresses, and Tracy rubs my back like she used to do when we were little. "Nope. Pretty sure this one's a panic attack."

I follow her through a couple of breathing exercises, straightening back up when it doesn't feel like I'm on the brink of passing out anymore. "What the hell? How could I possibly be in love with her? I barely know her."

Except, I feel like I do know her. Better than pretty much anyone else.

And it felt like she knew me, too. Like she really saw me.

Tracy shrugs. "Sorry. Love doesn't come with an instruction manual."

Silence fills the air for several beats.

"What the hell am I supposed to do now?"

"Well… Now you figure out what kind of idiot you are."

"What?"

"The way I see it, you can either be the idiot who gives up on something that could potentially be the best thing that's ever happened to him, or you could be the idiot who puts himself out there, even though there are no guarantees that she loves you back."

"Shit."

"Yep."

I heave a sigh. "Well, you'd better have some good ideas on how to win Lauren back, because you seriously give the worst pep talks."

Tracy's whoop is followed by Reece's footsteps thudding down the hall. "What are you guys doing? Can I be done playing with myself?"

"Yeah. I wish." Tracy shakes her head.

"Alright, Reece's Pieces." I pat the space next to me, and Reece scrambles up. "You remember Lauren?"

A wayward chunk of Reece's hair waves as he nods. "Uh-huh."

"Well, your Mom and I were about to figure out what to do to show her how much I like her. You got any ideas?"

Reece screws his face up. "Why don't you just tell her?"

"Simple. Effective. I like it." I give Reece a high five.

"Okay. That's a start. But I think you might want to up the ante just a bit," Tracy says. "Make it a little more memorable. You are Jake, after all, right?"

I give Tracy a blank stare.

"Go-big-or-go-home Jake? Death-defying, thrill-seeking Jake?"

"Or how about Superhero Jake?" Excitement lights Reece's eyes. "You could wear a costume and everything."

I open my mouth to let him know that I will definitely not be dressing up in Spandex or a cape, but close it as his suggestion triggers something that has potential. Something that's totally me, totally her, and totally embarrassing if it doesn't work.

Well, it's probably totally embarrassing even if it does work, but Tracy's right. If there ever was a time to go big or go home, it's now.

I just hope I don't wind up crashing like the last time I tried to go big.

Because I'm not sure I'd survive this one.

CHAPTER TWENTY-NINE

Lauren

Kylie wheels the customer's bike to the front of the shop. "Good as new, Stan. Remember to come in a little sooner next time. Those brakes don't last forever, you know."

The wiry, grey-haired man lifts an arm, displaying an impressive case of road rash. "Yeah, I know. And maybe if you keep nagging me, one day I'll finally remember to come in beforehand."

Kylie tilts her head. "You think if we added nagging to our service items, that might catch on?"

Stan shrugs. "If it keeps me from eating dirt and having to listen to Martha yell at me about it later, I'm in."

"Huh," I say, after Stan leaves. "That's a really good idea. Dentists and doctors send out reminder texts all the time. Why don't we?"

"Dad and I talked about it, but we never got around to it. It was on my to-do list, but then after he died…" The reminder of his death hangs in the air for several moments until she speaks again. "Thanks for helping me out again today."

"No problem." Especially since Jake's at his doctor's appointment and not coming back in today.

"Yeah, it *is* a problem."

"What?"

Kylie leans on the other side of the counter, her nose wrinkled. "It *is* a problem because you're right. You *are* always there for me. With Dad. And the shop. You're the glue that's holding this together right now. The glue that's holding *me* together. I know this isn't what you wanted." She swirls her hand through the air to indicate the shop. "You've given up a lot to help me keep it going. And I know I was hard on you with the whole Jake thing. And I'm sorry." She blows out a breath and gives me a hesitant smile. "Can you forgive me for being an ungrateful jackass?"

I swallow down the emotions vying to overtake my voice. "Yeah."

"Good. Because I'm gonna need all the help I can get in order to survive this co-bike program thing with Spence."

Yeah. She really is. In fact, maybe Aunt Sheila and I need to have a strategy session. Do some pre-planning for how to handle her when things go sideways.

Wait. Scratch that. No, we don't. We *don't* have to preplan for every little thing, because that's part of what I want to work on. *Not* planning several steps ahead. Taking things as they come. Loosening up.

Just like Jake.

My ribcage gets smaller as the thought sneaks into my brain once again.

Dammit. When is this gonna pass? When am I finally gonna put him out of my head and get on with my life?

"Speaking of Spence," Kylie continues. "Any chance you wanna help me kick his butt tonight?"

I snap my attention back to Kylie. "Depends. What are you guys competing for this time?"

"Well, he kinda challenged us to a karaoke sing-off tonight."

"Really? I didn't know Spencer can sing."

"He can't. Which is why I'm not really sure what his strategy is."

"Maybe his strategy is just to relax and have drinks and do some brainstorming about the bike program."

Kylie narrows her eyes. "Hmmm. Maybe."

I narrow *my* eyes, mirroring Kylie's suspicion, as an idea takes root. "Wait. Did you just apologize to me so I'd sing karaoke and you could beat Spencer?"

"What? No. I am perfectly capable of beating Spence on my own, thank you very much."

Oh, Lord. If Kylie thinks she's a better singer than Spencer, she's either got the whole delusional thing going again, or I should take earplugs. Maybe enough for the entire bar.

Either way, it should be entertaining. And I could use a little fun right about now.

As I follow Kylie across the bar toward Spencer's table, I make note of the usual suspects.

The Blue Hair ladies tittering amongst themselves at the table up front, Sonny and Cher cuddled up in a corner booth, and Mullet Mike nursing a beer at the bar. Huh. Looks like he got a new jumpsuit.

He raises his drink at me as I walk by. "Don't be cruel, now, you hear?"

"Um… Okay." Weird. Does he always talk in Elvis titles?

"Hey, ladies." Spencer grins and gestures to the empty seats. "Thanks for joining me."

"Thanks for the invite." Despite the fact that I'm trying not to, my eyes dart around the room. I'm not sure if I'm more relieved or disappointed when my Jake radar comes up empty.

Kylie slides into the chair across from Spence, and I slide into the seat between them as Spencer pours two beers from his pitcher. "Cheers." He raises his glass and waits as we do the same. "To the beginning of a beautiful relationship."

"Aw, Spencer. That's very thoughtful. Isn't it, Kylie?" I give her a pointed look.

"Yeah, yeah. Very thoughtful." She rolls her eyes and takes a healthy swallow of her drink.

Spencer winks. "What can I say? I'm a thoughtful kind of guy."

Kylie snorts. "Ow. Crap. That stings. Got beer up my nose."

I catch Spencer's eye, and he bites back a smile, quickly schooling his features when Kylie glares at him.

"So, Spencer," I say, "what are your thoughts on the whole co-winner thing?"

Spencer sips his beer. "Well, I have to admit it took me by surprise."

Kylie barks out a laugh. "Yeah. Join the club."

"But I think this could be a really good thing," he continues. "For all of us. And I'd rather be a co-winner than an all-out loser."

"Well then, you probably shouldn't have suggested a karaoke contest, sucker," Kylie says.

Spencer raises an eyebrow. "Please. Have you heard yourself sing? It's like listening to a bunch of cats in heat."

Kylie's nostrils flare. "What? Like you're any better. You couldn't carry a tune if it was in a suitcase."

Spencer shrugs. "Yeah, well, at least I'm not delusional. I am fully aware that I suck."

"I know I suck." Kylie shrugs. "I just suck with style."

The corner of Spencer's mouth ticks upward. "That's what I like about you. You admit that you suck, but you keep on doing it anyway. A lesser person would find that annoying."

"Hey!" Kylie scowls.

Spencer's attention shifts to something on the other side of the room, and he holds up a finger. "As much as I enjoy agreeing with you about how much you suck, we've got more important things to do right now." He juts his chin at something behind Kylie.

I follow his gaze and catch Mullet Mike making his way toward the stage.

Wait. That's not Mullet Mike.

That's Jake. In Mullet Mike's rhinestone jumpsuit.

Kylie turns in her seat. "What in the holy hell?"

My thoughts exactly.

Settling himself on his crutches, Jake pulls the microphone off the stand by the karaoke machine. His eyes lock onto mine, and my heart knocks against my ribs. Warmth curls low in my belly as he licks his lips. He takes a deep breath, blowing it out slowly as the first few notes of a slow ballad fill the bar.

And then he begins to sing.

His low, smooth voice sends pleasure jolts along my spine, and my breath catches as I realize why he's dressed like that. He's singing Elvis Presley's *Can't Help Falling in Love.*

Oh, my God. He's singing Elvis. In a rhinestone jumpsuit. About falling in love.

It's beautiful. And soulful. And, oh my God, I seriously can't breathe as he asks if he should stay.

Is this what I think it is? Is Jake really thinking about staying? And is he seriously telling me he's in love with me? In a song? In front of the whole bar?

Tears pool in my eyes, and I blink in an effort to contain them.

This is nuts. He's over me. Moved on. Moving away.

But if the song and the way he's singing it are to be believed, he's not.

Hope spreads its wings, and I work to swallow past the sudden thickening in my throat.

This is, by far and away, the craziest, sweetest, most unexpected thing that's ever happened to me. Kind of like Jake.

I sit, spellbound, until the final note fades.

The bar explodes into a mixture of catcalls, whistles, and thunderous applause.

"Thank you," Jake says, his Elvis imitation spot-on. "Thank you very much." He places the microphone back on the stand, winks at the Blue Hair table, then slowly makes his way off the stage.

"Wow," Kylie breathes. "That was…"

"Yeah." My pulse pounds in my ears as he crutches toward us.

Jake keeps his attention locked on me, a hesitant smile curving his mouth. "Hey."

"Hey."

Spencer pops up from his chair. "Great job, man. Kylie—can you come help me at the bar?"

"What? Why do you need help—"

Spencer rolls his eyes and tugs her shirt. "Just come with me."

"What? I don't want…" Understanding flashes across her face. "Oh. Right." Her eyes flick to Jake. "Your intentions here are honorable, right?"

Jake crosses his heart. "Completely."

Kylie nods and follows Spencer to the bar.

"Is this seat taken?" Jake gestures to one of the recently vacated chairs.

I shake my head, not trusting myself to try to string words together.

He sinks into the chair, his Adam's apple bobbing as he swallows. "Lauren, I have no idea what I'm doing. I think we can both agree that thinking things through is not my strong suit. And I know you're the complete opposite. That you've probably got the next ten years planned out. And I have no idea if I fit into your plans, but I'd really like to try." He rolls his lower lip between his teeth. "And I meant what I said up there. I have no idea exactly when it happened, and it still scares the shit out of me, but somewhere along the way, I fell in love with you." He sucks in a breath and blows it out. "Do you think we could try again?"

My head bounces up and down like a bobblehead. "I'd like that. A lot." I launch myself at him and attach my lips to his. Oh, damn, I've missed this. Missed him. The way his mouth feels against mine, the way our tongues work in tandem, the way we just seem to fit.

When we finally come up for air, Jake rests his forehead against mine. "Thank God. I was getting worried there for a few moments. Thought you were gonna tell me to fuck off."

"Are you kidding me? After what you just did? That was amazing." I lean back and run my gaze over his outfit. "And very sparkly."

The low rumble of his laugh sends the pleasure tingles racing through me again. "Yep. Go big or go home."

"So, does this mean you're staying?"

He nods.

"And does this mean you didn't move on?"

Confusion pinches his features.

"The picture from the bar? The brunette? Last week?"

"Oh." He grimaces. "Full disclosure? I went there trying to get you out of my system. But I couldn't. I think you broke me. That picture was for her nephew or cousin or something who's big into Motocross."

Wow. Aunt Sheila was right. "Okay. Full disclosure? I think you broke me, too. I was afraid I'd never be able to eat another hot fudge brownie sundae again."

Jake gasps. "The horrors!"

"I know. Scariest moments of my life." I bite my lip to try to keep my smile in check. "But seriously... I think we need some ground rules moving forward."

"Oh?"

"Yeah. I don't think I can abide by that whole 'honorable intentions' thing."

"No?"

"No. I think I'm gonna need at least ten percent dishonorable Jake."

The corners of his lips twitch. "Ten percent, huh?"

"Yep. Like, maybe Wild Wednesdays."

"Or Motorcycle Mondays?"

"Exactly."

He nods. "I think I can do that."

"I like your confidence."

He grins and leans forward, kissing me again. When he sits back, he shifts and stretches out his leg. A knee-high walking boot encases it.

"Oh, hey—you got your cast off!"

"Yep. Doc gave me the go-ahead to begin to put weight on it. If things go well, I should be able to get off the crutches in another couple of weeks."

"That's awesome."

Jake winks. "You're just saying that because you can't wait to ride me."

My face heats. "Oh, my God. You're never gonna let me live that down, are you?"

"Nope."

Tracy plops down into one of the empty seats, a smug look on her face. She takes a picture of us. "Speaking of things that are never getting lived down…" A grin stretches across her face as she eyeballs Jake's outfit.

"Hey!" Jake scowls. "I thought you said you were just gonna drop me off."

"What? And miss the chance to get action shots of you in this? I can't decide if I want to use them for this year's Christmas cards or for blackmail." She taps her chin. "Decisions, decisions."

"Hey, Tracy." I give her a little wave.

Tracy's gaze bounces back and forth between us, an expectant smile on her face. "So, I take it from that kiss that you two are thinking of getting the band back together?"

I look at Jake, then nod.

She lets out a squeal and does a shoulder shimmy. "Yay! We have so much to talk about. Did you know he used to like to wear his underwear overtop of his pants?"

I cock an eyebrow. "No. I was not aware of that fact."

Jake shrugs. "It's all the rage with superheroes."

Kylie and Spencer pull up additional chairs and sit down. "Is it safe to come back?" Spencer asks. "Or are we interrupting something?"

"Only my sister," Jake says. "Thanks for helping out, man." He fist-bumps Spencer.

"My pleasure."

"Help?" I ask.

"Yep. Spencer was in charge of getting you here tonight."

Spencer winks. "You're welcome."

"See?" Kylie jabs a finger at him. "I *told* you he had an agenda." She huffs out a breath, a reluctant smile playing at her lips. "But I guess it's okay this time." Her expression softens even further. "If this is what you want, then I'm happy for you."

Tears prick my eyes again, and I turn my attention back to Jake. "Yeah. This is exactly what I want."

I didn't know it, but this is exactly what I've always wanted.

To feel like the best version of me.

To be pushed outside of my box.

To feel free.

CHAPTER THIRTY

Jake

Tracy dusts her hands and stretches out her back. "Alright, I think that's the last one."

"Thanks, guys." I look around my apartment. For someone who's lived as a nomad, I sure do have a lot of shit. Boxes are stacked against the living room wall and on the kitchen counter, and last I saw, my bedroom was littered with duffel bags. I got a decent deal on a couch and recliner, Tracy and Craig foisted their old coffee table and dining set on me, and Lauren's Aunt Sheila practically paid me to take a dresser and an assortment of end tables and kitchen stuff. Despite the fact that it's still a mess, a sense of peace washes over me.

This feels right.

Reece hops from one foot to the other. "Can I sleep over?"

"Sure, Reece's Pieces. But, uh, not tonight, okay?" My eyes dart to Lauren. I have plans for someone to help me christen my new bed, and it's not my nephew.

Lauren's cheeks flush as Reece's shoulders slump.

"I promise that you and I are gonna have lots of sleepovers, okay, buddy?"

Reece nods, but his little shoulders look like he's carrying the weight of the world.

"Come on." Tracy ruffles his hair. "For being such a big helper today, what say we go get some ice cream?"

"Okay." His face lights up. "Can I get sprinkles?"

"Absolutely." Tracy sighs, a wistful look on her face. "Ah, to have the attention span of a flea." She looks around my place and nods. "You did a really good job picking this place out. I like it."

"Thanks." I wink at Lauren. "It was a joint effort."

"Well, you two definitely make a good team."

"Yeah, we do," I say.

Yet another thing that feels right—being with her. Before getting injured, I never would've pictured myself being happy settling down in one place, let alone with one woman.

But now I can't imagine anything else.

After Tracy drags Reece away, I lock the door, leaning against it to get some of the weight off my leg. Lauren frowns. "I told you not to push it so hard today. How bad is it?"

"Uncomfortable, but nothing I can't handle." In truth, I probably should've used my crutches, but I really hate those things. "And I'm pretty sure a good therapy session tonight will help. A lot." I limp over and wrap my arms around her. "Maybe two therapy sessions. I'm a mess."

She draws her head away from me, her nose wrinkled. "Yeah, and you're not smelling so hot right now, either."

"I thought you liked my man sweat."

"Not when we have that fabulous tub in that fabulous bathroom of your fabulous new apartment." She waggles her eyebrows.

"I knew I liked you."

She runs her hands under my T-shirt and shimmies it up and over my head, tossing it to the floor. "Yeah, well, right back atcha. Now come on… Less talking and more walking." Grabbing my hand, she drags me to the bathroom.

"Damn, woman. Keep it in your pants."

"Are you sure that's really what you want?"

"Nope. Not at all. Forget I said that. In fact, get out of your pants. Right now."

She bites her bottom lip, keeping her eyes on mine as she wiggles her hips, slowly teasing her shorts down.

"Oh, my God. Get there faster."

"Slow down there, speedy. Good things take time."

"You're killing me. Or at least causing potential brain damage, seeing as how my blood is nowhere near my head right now."

Her gaze dips to the tenting in my shorts, and the flush on her cheeks intensifies. "Yeah. I can see that."

A wicked smile curves her lips as she continues her slow, sexy striptease, and I growl. "Fine. But don't say I didn't warn you." Crossing to her, I press her against the counter and yank off her shirt. Her bra follows. Oh, sweet Jesus. I will never get tired of her perfect breasts.

She purrs as I use my tongue and fingers to show them how much I admire them.

"Bathtub. Now. Please," she pants.

"I thought you'd never ask."

Following several spectacular christenings of my new tub, I relax, Lauren sprawled on top of me like a limp noodle.

Damn. I didn't think it was possible, but every time with Lauren just keeps getting better. I never knew something like that was possible.

"Oh—remind me to update the website with the new children's program," Lauren mumbles against my chest.

"How can you even think about that right now?"

"Big brain. I'm multitasking."

"*Of course* you are." Even though she's now being more vocal about what she wants, Lauren's still knee-deep in the shop. Between the two of us, the new programs are really starting to shape up. Sessions for kids, like what I did for Reece, individual and group sessions for adults, and a new cycling and stress relief program with Tracy and Kylie.

And, of course, there's the new City program, which is a whole other beast. While I think it has the potential to be really good, it'll be a miracle if both Kylie and Spencer make it through alive. If the shop wasn't so heavily dependent on it, it would probably be fun just to sit back and watch the fireworks.

I trace the butterflies on her back. "Thank you."

"You're welcome." She cocks her head and peels open an eyelid. "For what?"

"For being you. And showing me who I really am. Who I can be. I know you think I broadened your horizons, but believe me, you broadened mine, too." I kiss the top of her head.

"While we're on the subject, I should thank you, too." She snuggles against me and places her hand over my heart. "You make me feel like I can soar."

I clear my throat, suddenly thick with emotion. "And you feel like coming home."

THE END

*Excited to see what happens with Kylie and Cycle Moore? Stay tuned for book two in the Shifting into Love series, **GEARING UP**.*

AUTHOR BIO & WHERE TO FIND ME

Roseanne Beck is an award-winning author of romantic comedies whose writing style has been described as "witty and funny and a little bit sexy."

She loves to make things awkward for her characters, and her stories tend to feature strong, flawed women, injured men, and a hint of the paranormal.

Physician by day, she uses of mixture of writing, laughter, and 80s music to help relieve stress.

If you enjoyed this book, please consider leaving a review on Amazon or Goodreads.

Find Roseanne at

Facebook

Twitter

BookBub

Goodreads

Or sign up for her newsletter here

SNEAK PEEK: GEARING UP

Kylie

People in love are idiots.

Case in point—the man in the rhinestone Elvis jumpsuit and the woman currently trying to suck his face off.

Granted, I happen to know those particular idiots. Hell, I'm related to one of them. The blonde face-sucker at the table on the other side of the bar is my younger sister, Lauren, and sparkly Elvis is our bike mechanic, Jake.

My gut twists, chagrin and happiness folding together like a vanilla and chocolate swirl of soft serve.

I'm happy for them. I am. Lauren deserves it. Especially for putting up with me and my crap over the past year. As if our dad dying and me leaning heavily on her to help out with the shop wasn't enough, I've also had my head up my ass since my latest breakup.

Scratch that. My *final* breakup. Because after the whole AJ fiasco, I'm done with men.

My fingers curl around my beer bottle at the thought of my ex. The no-good, cheating son of a bitch. How the hell did I not see that he was messing around with *his* ex?

I'm such an idiot.

Spence nudges me with his elbow.

"What?" I growl.

Instead of being put off by my patented laser-beam death glare, he just grins.

Idiot.

"You know… I meant what I said back there." He tips his head toward the lovebirds.

"You mean the part about knowing that you suck?" While it's true that he can't sing, I never expected him to actually admit it.

He shrugs. "Well, that, and the part about us co-winning being a good thing."

For about the tenth time in as many weeks I wonder what I did to piss the universe off so royally.

As if I didn't have enough on my plate with the upcoming anniversary of Dad's death and trying to figure out how to get our bike shop through the next few months financially, now I've gotta deal with Spence and the whole City Bike Program thing.

I know I should be glad that we won, and I am. Mostly. The grant money will definitely help, as will the monthly stipend and the increased marketing visibility. But the fact that we're co-winners with Spence's shop takes some of the luster off the whole winning aspect. Partly because it means we'll be splitting the money, and partly because, well, it's *Spence*.

He nudges me again. "Admit it. You're excited about it."

"Yeah," I mutter. "About as excited as if I was getting my toenails surgically removed."

"Hey, whatever floats your boat."

I roll my eyes and take another swig of beer. A lifetime ago, Spence himself had floated my boat. But those days are long gone.

Unfortunately, the idiot beside me lingers on.

"We should probably set up some times to get together," he continues. "You know... check each other out." He keeps his gray-green eyes on mine, lifting one eyebrow ever-so-slightly while the corner of his mouth angles upward into the ghost of a smile.

A lifetime ago, that stupid smirk would've given me an adrenaline rush to rival the time I hit the game-winning basket to win Regionals in high school. Now, however, it elicits another eye roll. "Let's be perfectly clear. I am not now, nor will I ever be, interested in checking you out."

He gives me a long-suffering look. "I *meant* we should check out each other's shops. For the program. You know, get to know each other's strengths and weaknesses. But hey, if you want to check me out..." The smirk returns.

Jackass.

A squeal from the direction of Jake and Lauren catches my attention. Jake's sister, Tracy, has interrupted their love fest. Thank God. Because the longer it's just me and Spence, the higher the chance of my hand reaching up to slap the smirk off his face.

And I really can't afford an assault charge.

With another laser death glare, I grab my beer and stalk across the bar, dropping into one of the empty seats at the table. Spence had dragged me away after Jake did his sparkly Elvis impersonation and proclaimed his love to Lauren via karaoke.

Another pang hits me. Now that I've gotten used to the idea, they really are perfect for each other. Lauren's loosened up immensely, and Jake fits in with our little operation rather seamlessly.

Huh. Hopefully this means he's sticking around now, and I don't have to keep searching for a new mechanic.

Bonus!

My uplifted spirits take another nosedive when Spence plops down beside me, the same stupid grin on his face. "Is it safe to come back?" he asks. "Or are we interrupting something?"

"Only my sister," Jake says. "Thanks for helping out, man." He fist-bumps Spence.

"My pleasure."

"Help?" Lauren asks, her eyes bouncing between Jake and Spence.

Jake nods. "Yep. Spencer was in charge of getting you here tonight."

Spence winks at Lauren. "You're welcome."

"See?" I jab a finger at Spence, directing my words to Lauren. "I *told* you he had an agenda." My initial sense of victory about being right collides with the fact that his sneakiness was for Lauren's greater good.

Dammit.

I huff out a breath, my irritation slipping further as I catch the tender look in Jake's eyes and the pure love on Lauren's face. "But I guess it's okay this time. If this is what you want, then I'm happy for you."

Lauren blinks, her eyes shiny. "Yeah. This is exactly what I want."

Tracy sighs and places a hand over her heart, and just for a moment, I feel little fingers of envy clawing at me. That Lauren's found someone who completes her. Who gets her. Who makes her a better version of herself.

"Jealousy does not become you," Spence murmurs, his breath hot on my neck.

I jump. But only because I wasn't expecting him to be so close. Not because he still seems to have the knack for getting inside my brain. "I'm not jealous."

The corner of his mouth lifts. "Right. You keep telling yourself that." Louder, he adds, "Now, I do believe there's still the matter of you, me, and a karaoke competition." He wags his finger between the two of us before pointing toward the stage.

The word *competition* yanks me back from the edge of envy and self-pity. "You're on. What are the stakes?"

He squints as if in deep thought, the smirk teasing the corners of his lips once again. "Loser has to post daily on social media and their website about how great the other bike shop is, and how deserving they are for the Best Of award."

My fingers tighten around my beer bottle. If only it was Spence's neck. He's won that damn award for the past three years. A fact that pisses me off to no end. Which he knows full well.

And he also knows full well that while I'm good at many things, singing isn't one of them. Which, if I were competing against anyone else, would be a problem. But this is Spence. And he sucks just as much as I do. Maybe more. If we teamed up for a duet, we'd probably be able to clear the bar out in under ten seconds.

But as much as that would certainly be entertaining to watch, Spence and I will most definitely *not* be teaming up for any duets. Because he is Spence.

And I must crush him.

ALSO BY ROSEANNE BECK

TALK TO ME

LOVE HURTS SERIES:

TURN THE PAIGE
SINGLE BY DESIGN
MEDITATE ON THIS

SHIFTING INTO LOVE SERIES:

GEARING UP

Made in the USA
San Bernardino, CA
25 July 2020